I'm Will

William Haylon

iUniverse, Inc.
Bloomington

I'm Will

This is a work of fiction. All of the characters, names, incidents,
organizations, and dialogue in this novel are either the products
of the author's imagination or are used fictitiously.
iUniverse books may be ordered through booksellers or by contacting:
iUniverse
1663 Liberty Drive
Bloomington, IN 47403
www.iuniverse.com
1-800-Authors (1-800-288-4677)

Because of the dynamic nature of the Internet, any web addresses or links contained in this
book may have changed since publication and may no longer be valid. The views expressed
in this work are solely those of the author and do not necessarily reflect the views of the
publisher, and the publisher hereby disclaims any responsibility for them.

Any people depicted in stock imagery provided by Thinkstock are models,
and such images are being used for illustrative purposes only.
Certain stock imagery © Thinkstock.

ISBN: 978-1-4759-4709-0 (sc)
ISBN: 978-1-4759-4710-6 (hc)
ISBN: 978-1-4759-4711-3 (e)

Library of Congress Control Number: 2012917387

Printed in the United States of America

iUniverse rev. date: 9/13/2012

Prologue

I FOUND THE PARTICULAR wood bench that I had been looking for by an old stone wall in the back behind the Fort. It was nice to sneak off here by myself and simply enjoy sitting alone in the warm, lazy sun of late spring, away from all the revelry. Still saddled with the tie and jacket dictated by the events of the day, it didn't take long before small beads of sweat began to wander aimlessly down the side of my head, past where my sideburns had already started to turn gray, until I could watch them drip into the grass between my spread legs. The last time I'd sat on this bench was probably the lowest moment of my entire life. I could only smile now.

The Fort stood atop a hill from which I could see seemingly endless playing fields stretched out beneath me. I watched as a handful of men finished disassembling the white canvas tent that had covered the portable stage used for the morning's ceremony. The chore of closing up the several hundred metal folding chairs, where my family had been seated just hours before, and returning them to the rental truck was almost complete. The litter of discarded programs and empty plastic water bottles had been collected neatly into large green trash bags and would soon be headed for the dumpsters behind the hockey rink. With the exception of the trampled grass of what was usually left field, any hint of the event would be gone by dinner.

Beyond left field, the playing fields remained an unflawed quilt of emerald due to the unusually heavy spring rains. On the lower field, at the far corner of the school's property, next to the creek that was a last tiny artery of the Charles River this far west of Boston, a sole working man pushed a lawnmower about the infield grass of one of the baseball diamonds. I watched the man with the lawnmower slowly weave repeatedly smaller squares about the infield, careful not to blow the grass trimmings onto the dirt, lest he be back in a month to pull new sprouts from the base paths for which grass wasn't intended. I somehow remembered that his name was Louis. Like my father, Louis was physically sturdy from his life of hard labor. He laconically walked behind his mower, his bowed legs rocking his rounded shoulders from side to side as he went. He was well into his fifties, and he had been here for a long time. I knew that Louis's son also worked here on the grounds crew. But that was all I knew about Louis. For him it was another working day, no different from any other. In the basic gray t-shirt and green polyester workman's pants of those never destined for higher education, he would toil in the early season sun until his next break when he could have another Coke and a cigarette. I could quite easily sit here for another couple of hours and watch Louis grind away. His laps around the diamond were mesmerizing. Louis and his son would be here again tomorrow to carry out some other tasks that to most of us had been invisible over the past four years.

My son's graduation had been over for more than three hours. An impressive crowd of people had come. Comfortably tanned grandparents had made the trek from Florida or the Cape. All the immodest parents had arrived early, ready to recount to anyone who would listen all the colleges to which their privileged children had been accepted. The bored-to-tears siblings were ready to go home before they had even arrived. And, of course, there were the newly minted graduates eager to begin what I suspected would be four years of primal college partying a few months early. They were all beginning now to disband. They had come buoyed by the triumphant spirit of this day that we had all been looking forward to for so many years, but they had been here long enough, and it had come time for them to go. Still, I was content just sitting here alone,

After four long years, I realized that I could finally exhale.

Four years ago, my wife and I had decided that our eldest son, Will, should go to a selective private high school in the Boston area where we lived. We assumed that smaller classes, higher teacher expectations, and ostentatious campuses would help him realize his many abilities that had been mostly dormant up to that point in his life. Get him out of his comfort zone. Not settle for less than he should. This would be a big financial sacrifice for us, but we weren't going to let other kids Will's age get a head start over him. Fortunately—although given the ultimate experience I'm not actually certain this is the correct choice of words— one of the many schools to which he'd applied actually let him in.

I had come from a truly humble background. My parents were blue collar through and through, but they had established an admirable foundation for all of their children that had been based upon strong work ethic and good values. Family meals, jobs after school, proper homework rituals, early to bed. My brothers, sisters, and I all went to public schools. We'd worked our way through college and had gotten financial aid and scholarships to fill the holes. Those same character traits my parents had imparted to us remained with me long after my academic life was completed. When my wife and I began a family, we hoped more than anything our kids would share the same discipline so they would be able to compete in this increasingly complicated world. The reality is that I probably started thinking about college for Will when he was in first or second grade. I didn't want any of my kids left behind.

I remember being pretty excited when we sent Will off for that first day at his exclusive new high school, convinced that this was the magical solution to his academic indifference. Over the next four years, he physically grew a foot, added tens of pounds, developed a dusting of facial hair, and completed something like six hundred nights of homework. Sometimes he even did the work of his own initiative and without my incessant prodding. I can't say it turned out to be the favorite four years of his life. It certainly wasn't for me.

I think that high school can be a difficult time for a lot of kids. It seemed it was even more of a challenge for Will. He seemed to find ways to do dumb things without even trying. Some were reasonably trivial; others were a little more daunting. And, I suspect that I knew only half or so of his misdeeds. Heck, by the end of high school, Will had managed to be on a first name basis with the school psychologist even though there was really nothing wrong with him. Though a few of the other parents may ultimately disagree, I think Will is basically a good person. Just maybe a little misguided sometimes.

Will's high school years certainly brought out the worst in me as well. It was more stressful than anything I could have possibly imagined. And somewhere along the way, I think I lost my focus on what it meant to be a good father. Not something that made me particularly proud.

After reflecting for a little while longer, I finally stood and removed my tie and jacket, laying them safely on the grass beneath me. I rolled up my sleeves and set off down the hill toward the baseball field. I expected that Louis might find some help both welcome and amusing. Four long years, a hundred twenty thousand or so dollars that I'm not certain were worth it, and I was going to go mow grass. As I headed down the hill towards where the maintenance man was working, I figured that at forty-four years old, it might be time for me to get back to my roots. It might be a good lesson for me to learn while I was still here.

I wonder if the school would have reconsidered its decision to accept Will given what they know about him now. He certainly surprised us all in many ways. So maybe yes. But, then again, maybe no. But I guess, in reality, I am hoping for the latter. I figure I still have two more sons to try to get into this damned place.

CLASS IV

STARTING HIGH SCHOOL ISN'T easy, particularly when your parents pull you out of the familiar public school system where you've spent your entire, mediocre academic life up until then, and drop you off at an expensive new private school with the intention of your immediately discovering a new intellectual discipline.

It was clear to me from the moment I stepped through the entrance that I wasn't ever likely to be comfortable at this place. I certainly never would have even applied to the school if it had been my decision to make. Even the seemingly basic stuff was not at all inspiring. The blazer they made us wear, for example, became my straightjacket. And except for maybe Christmas and my grandfather's funeral, I'd never even had to wear a tie to church. Now I'd have to wear one every day. It took me something like fifteen tries in the morning to make a decent knot.

The cramped auditorium was already filled with boys in the same bland uniform. Wall to wall blue blazers. Most had white oxford shirts like mine; a few had blue or stripes. Some shirttails hung below the blazers. Overly baggy khaki pants were everywhere. And if we had ever been allowed to unbutton our shirts, the boxers on every single one of us in the room would have been seen to be yanked up three inches above our belts. We went to a lot of effort and spent a ton of money to look so much alike.

The girls were almost as xeroxed as we were. Tight button-down blouses, the bottoms of which were often not even in the same zip code as the waists of their skirts. And the skirts, in and of themselves, were the true genius of physics. How the waists hung so low without showing any butt crack could, ultimately, be one of the greatest unsolved mysteries of my overestimated generation. We always looked, but we never saw. South of the border, every skirt in the room tested what I soon learned was the "dollar rule"— the distance from the top of the knee to the edge of the skirt could be no more than the length of a dollar bill. Cleavage was volunteered and obvious, whether it was warranted or not.

From my insignificant roost on the back edge of the gradually descending sea of auditorium seating, I could see them all. So many already seemed so familiar with one another as they roamed in small factions in search of their prescribed places to sit. There were only maybe four hundred kids in the Upper School, and as they piecemeal found their destinations, they crammed comfortably into the worn brown pull-down seats. The faculty, an odd bunch in their own right, sat in metal folding chairs up on the small stage. Young, baby faced teachers full of energy and nerves. Some were only a couple of years out of college and, hence, were no more than a half dozen years more grown up than the oldest kids in the audience. If they thought they were ready to open our minds to the curiosities of the world around us, they were overly optimistic. We weren't that deep. It wouldn't take too many years before they'd be just like the older faculty. Teachers we had worn out. Teachers who knew their lesson plans by heart and were now trying to figure out how they were going to afford college tuition for their own children after teaching for so many years for what amounted to not much more than minimum wage. The whole school in a single room. At my old school, maybe a single grade had a chance of fitting in here.

My old school had an inhospitable but memorable odor each fall when the academic year began. Hallway walls had the patented fragrance of yet another fresh coat of paint completed days before the first classes began. Floors, too worn to shine any longer, would nonetheless reek of cleaning fluid and generic wax. Even the toilets in the bathrooms had those little round bars that made the water blue and kept the smell from being offensive, at least for the first day or two. This place had none of that smell. It just smelled different. And because it smelled different, it was not at this moment a welcoming place. Frankly, the whole thing scared the hell out of me.

"New?"

I hadn't been in any hurry to start the new school year and had assumed I'd been the last to arrive, but apparently there was someone who had cut it even closer than I had.

"Is it that obvious?"

"Yeah. I actually don't recognize you."

"I'm Will."

"You're class four?"

"What?"

"You're a freshman?"

"That's right."

"I don't remember ever seeing you here before today."

"I'm new here. It's my first day."

"Yeah, but you weren't at the orientation cookout for new kids last spring, were you?"

"No. I just got in off the wait list this summer."

"Mmm."

"You don't make it sound like such a good thing."

"That you didn't show up at orientation?"

"No. I was thinking more about getting in off the wait list."

"I guess it's better than not getting in at all but worse than getting in on time."

I'd gone to public school my whole life. I had thought that I was doing reasonably well; my parents thought I lacked initiative.

"What's your name?"

"I'm Hartford."

"That's your name?"

"Yup."

"Are you new here, too?" I asked.

"No. Been here since seventh grade."

"Where do you live?"

"In the Fort."

"You're named after a city, and you live in a fort?"

"It's the big old stone building at the bottom of the hill."

"You live at the school?"

"Don't you?"

"No. I actually didn't know that kids boarded here. I live at home with my family."

"Mmm."

"Do you like living here?"

"It's alright."

"How are the rooms?"

"Decent."

"How about the food?"

"Edible on good days."

"Do you have to do your own laundry?"

"Yeah, that kinda sucks."

"It's funny. I don't really even know how to do laundry."

"I didn't either until I got here."

"Mmm." I nodded in agreement even though I didn't really have any idea why I should be nodding.

My parents used to brag about me to their friends. I had overheard the conversations many times. But when it was just me around, I suddenly became a slug. Fixated on television, no help around the house, hidden in class. Frankly, I couldn't argue with them, but it was a little confusing nonetheless.

"Did you get your syllabus?"

"I don't know."

"You don't know?"

"I don't know what that is."

"A syllabus?"

"Right."

"You've never had a syllabus before at school?"

"I don't think I could even spell the word."

"S-y-l-l-a-b-u-s."

"I was right."

"It's a list that tells you the homework each night for the whole term."

"The whole term?"

"Even the days you have tests or papers due."

"Really?"

"Mmm."

"Man, I got a lot to learn."

So they decided that I should apply to private schools in the spring of eighth grade. Roxbury Latin, Belmont Hill, BB&N (which stood for something I could never remember), Middlesex, Groton, St. Mark's, Brooks, Pendleton Academy, Rivers. These were supposedly all of the best private schools in the Boston area where I lived. I toured from school to school, interviewing in my blue blazer and answering questions about where I wanted to go to college and what I was hoping to do with my life. Usually I was just hoping to go home and eat lunch. Maybe play a video game. But my parents seemed to know what I wanted. They pressed on until I had completed interviews and campus tours at all nine schools.

"Is the work here hard?"

"Not too bad. Maybe a little harder for you since you're off the wait list."

"Are the kids here really smart?"

"Some are really smart. Some are just really rich."

"Which are you?"

"Maybe a little of each."

"You didn't get in off the wait list, huh?

"Hardly."

So I applied to all the schools. My parents wrote some great essays for me. But when the acceptances came, I hadn't gotten into any of them. Zero for nine. One school put me on its wait list. So the revised plan was that I would go to the public high school, which was fine with me. That was where all my friends were going.

"What's your old man do?"

"He works for a company that sells some kind of medical software. How about yours?"

"He's the governor."

"Governor of what?"

"Massachusetts."

"No kidding?"

"No kidding."

"I guess that's a pretty good job."

"It has its benefits."

"So are they strict here?"

"Only if you get lousy grades. Or if you get caught drinking or smoking."

"Mmm."

"Or getting a blow job."

"Mmmm."

I nodded again.

"Exactly."

"I guess I had better go try to find my silly thing."

"Syllabus."

"Yeah, that too."

My mother got a call on August 15th. Pendleton Academy—or Pendy, as it was called—was going to let me in off its wait list. Somebody had dropped out at the last minute; the husband hadn't gotten a large enough bonus so they could no longer afford the thirty thousand dollar annual tuition. The school needed an answer the next day. We talked about it that night as a family. My folks told me to sleep on it; it would be my choice. The next morning they made me go to Pendy.

"Better hurry. They don't like us loitering back here. Classes start five minutes after assembly. You probably didn't know you have a paper due today."

"The first day?"

"From the summer reading list. You'll learn."

"I don't even have any books yet."

"Man, you really are behind. Just go online to the school website. You can print the list of stuff you need from your laptop."

"I don't have a laptop."

"You don't?"

"Do I need one?"

"You pretty much have to have one."

"They're kind of expensive."

"I suppose."

"I better call my parents."

"Here. You can borrow my cell."

2.

We lived in the town of Wellesley, a sort of suburban Mafia enclave of upscale families known for a prestigious women's college by the same name and lots of McMansions. It was a town where people bought homes because it supposedly had a really good public school system. But by the time the kids became school age, a huge percentage applied to private schools. I could never understand why parents would send a kid to a private kindergarten or first grade. In my mind, there wasn't much that a smaller class size or nicer desks could do to impact finger painting. But in Wellesley they sent them anyway.

We weren't as rich as most of the families in town, but my dad worked hard to make sure we did okay. It was actually one of the few things I admired about him. Our house was similar to many of the others in town. From the outside it looked pretty much like a postcard. Inside it was a museum. We did all of our living in the kitchen and a big family room, while the other rooms stood carefully ornamented and empty, waiting for the single annual party we threw every New Year's Eve. Outside, all the trees and shrubs were as if someone had digitally arranged them. And the grass seemed as if nobody had ever walked on it, which may have been true because we spent so much time playing video games on the ever bigger television in the family room.

Most of the work to keep everything looking so great was done by a crew of Brazilian men who came around every week or so to trim bushes, put down fertilizer, mow the grass, or plow the snow. I always felt bad for these men. Their faces changed from year to year, but they all worked hard, and their features were permanently creased from the summer sun and winter wind, and they perpetually looking so tired and dirty. Their hands were like lizard skin from making a living with shovels, rakes, hedge trimmers, and leaf blowers. They were well past the point of ever needing work gloves. I was less than half the age of most of them. I should have been calling them "sir" and working for them. But because they spoke only Portuguese and I spoke only English, we never really discussed the topic. Every once in a while, I would bring them some cold lemonade or hot chocolate. They would politely nod, sip the refreshment, and hand me back the cup. I was probably as much a mystery to them as they were to me.

But with the new school my focus was elsewhere those first few days of September. I usually felt nauseous by the time I came down to the kitchen in the morning. Even dry Cheerios made me sick. After the first couple of days, I just stopped eating breakfast altogether. Still, the unsettling churning of my stomach would stay with me throughout the ride to school and into the start of the day. Each morning of the week began in the auditorium with what they called assembly. Assembly was where the faculty and the student leaders made the announcements of all of the upcoming activities—and there were a lot of them. Once in a while, as I later discovered, they would extend assembly to allow for some supposedly well-known guest speaker. Of course, I had never heard of any of them. Mr. Bussmann, the dean of students, got most of the faculty airtime. Buzzsaw, as many of the kids called him behind his back, was also the dean of discipline. Short, at least a hundred pounds overweight, and with the permanent stench of a closet smoker, he was rumored to be a pretty good guy except when he lost his temper. Thus the nickname. Most of the student leaders were seniors. Even though we were all at the same school, they seemed to exist on a plane entirely different from mine. Somehow the appearance of sideburns or boobs, depending upon their sides of the gender fence, brought with it a level of self-confidence that I was certain I would never enjoy.

My allotted seat was almost exactly in the center of the auditorium. The big anxiety each morning was that, given my seasick stomach, I would blow cookies in the middle of the whole school before I could get to a bathroom. There was an ugly obstacle course of khaki covered male and barely covered female legwork between seat L32 and the toilet. I so feared barfing in front of the entire student population that I rarely caught what was being said by any of the speakers. Instead, I would chew on my lower lip, focus every non-nauseous cell in my body on trying to keep down the contents of my stomach, and contemplate which of the limbs in my path might cause the biggest impediment in any obligatory sprint to safety that particular morning. I was deathly afraid of the potential of a splash landing in the lap of some badass senior guy. Or of a girl classmate in a skirt that didn't meet the dollar rule.

By the end of the first class, my insides would have by and large calmed down, but for the rest of those early days my understanding of the inner workings of my unsettling new institution lagged a little behind the rest of the students because I hadn't really heard the morning's broadcasts. On the second day I missed the sign ups for clubs. Not that I had planned to join any, but I didn't have a particularly compelling answer when my father asked about them. Day three I missed the sign-up for sports. I was the deaf kid in the land of great talkers.

"Sign up was yesterday, Will."

"Sorry, Coach. I didn't hear the announcement."

Coach, the real story is that I was using every bit of courage and conviction I had not to puke on your star quarterback who was sitting in front of me.

"You need to pay better attention."

"Yes, sir."

"You want to play football?"

"I was hoping to."

"Most of the kids have already been here for a couple of weeks for preseason camp."

"I got in off the wait list, Coach."

"You're pretty small, Will."

I seemed to be the smallest damned kid in the whole Upper School. Half the boys in my class already shaved. One apparently even had his learner's permit. Ultimately I learned what "redshirting" meant. Kids in public schools are never held back unless they are in unbelievable trouble—and even then the teachers usually still passed them along to the next grade so as not to have to deal with them again. Here the kids stayed back to get bigger for sports. Even most of the girls could probably kick my butt. Five foot four, one hundred and fifteen pounds. But everybody had to play a sport or do some other after-school activity every season, which was fine by me as I'd always loved sports.

"I'm tougher than I look. And I'm pretty fast."

"Well I'm glad to hear that. Why don't you try cross-country? I don't want to see you get hurt."

Cross-country? That's not even a sport!

"I'd like to give football a try, sir."

"Why don't you come out next year—at the proper registration time. We'll see if you're a little bigger by then."

This was going to suck.

So I reluctantly showed up for cross-country practice the next day. The single upside of the experience was that I met the kid who would become my first friend at the school. He was big, fat—easily twice my size—and black. He came in a warm-up jacket, high top sneakers, camouflage cargo pants, a sideways baseball cap, and all kinds of attitude.

"You sure you in the ninth grade?"

"Yeah, why?" I replied.

"You kinda small."

"That's what everybody keeps telling me."

"I'm Shaky."

"I'm Will."

He didn't stick out his hand to shake, so I didn't stick out mine.

"Is that your real name?" I asked.

"Real 'nuff."

"How long have you been going here?"

"My first year."

"Me too."

"How come I ain't seen you before?"

"I can be kind of invisible."

"That's hard for me to do," Shaky laughed, rubbing his abundant midsection.

"Are you one of the rich kids or the smart kids?" I asked.

"I ain't neither."

"You're not?"

"Nope. I'm black. But I know what you're saying. I live in a poor part 'a Boston. They got to let a few 'a us in for diversity sake."

"You're pretty big. How come you don't play football?"

"Truthfully?"

"Mmm."

"I don't want anybody tackling my ass. I ain't a big fan 'a pain."

"Wait till you try running three and a half miles."

"Won't be no problem. I'll fake a injury if I got to."

The cross-country coach told Shaky he needed to get some better clothes to run in. So the next day Shaky showed up with expensive running shoes and designer running shorts, along with the sideways baseball cap and the attitude. I discovered from him a few days later that some athletic store in Boston would have found itself minus a few items that week if it counted its inventory. But being an outsider in both this world and that one, I wasn't about to tell anybody.

There were sixteen of us in total. Some of the runners were pretty strong. Others were pretty awful. Shaky wasn't the only misfit in our group. Edmund, or Fast Eddie, as we later called him, wore the waistband of his running shorts up around his chest. Dawson, who wasn't much taller than me, was just as skinny and spent most of each practice picking his nose. He actually sat in seat L31 during assembly—right next to me. He arrived to his seat before me every morning but so far hadn't said boo. He was apparently the youngest of six in an impressively wealthy family, all of whom had gone to Pendy, and he would prove by the end to be more screwed up than most.

Each afternoon our group of runners would take to the paths through the woods around the school's 198 acre campus, Eddie with his permanent wedgie, Dawson and his nose claw, and our out-of-shape black rapper in his designer running clothes trailing the pack while cursing aloud to anyone who would listen. The campus was truly different from anything I had ever seen before. First off, at public schools nobody ever used the term "campus." Second, there was a maze of buildings here—as opposed to the massive single old brick and cement structure that we all had gotten lost in during our first week of middle school. The school was built on a property just west of Boston proper. It had apparently been originally located within the city boundaries, but moved further out shortly after World War I to gain access to more land. The main entrance to the school was next to a small building that housed a psychiatric practice, something I always found humor in. It sort of kept things in perspective.

The epicenter of the campus was an L-shaped building named Gooden Hall, but which everyone called the Main School, all having long ago forgotten who Gooden was. The majority of the classrooms resided in the Main School, as did the admissions office, where potential students were interviewed. I had interviewed there with my parents only a few months before. With new sofas, overstuffed chairs, oriental rugs, and antique lamps, it was by far the nicest area in the entire school. But the peculiar quiet of frightened students and stressed parents—more quiet than the library—brought back unsettling memories. When I found out that only 147 of the 952 kids who applied were actually accepted, I didn't feel as badly about getting in off the wait list. Still, I had no real interest in setting foot in the admissions office during the rest of my time at Pendy.

Science and art were housed in a separate, more modern building next door. They seemed a strange combination of subjects to me. One building beyond was the middle school for sixth, seventh, and eighth graders, but we never saw or interacted with them. These were the kids who'd gone to private school in kindergarten to perfect becoming finger-painting prodigies. Their parents were maniacal about getting them into prestigious colleges no matter what the price. They were determined to avoid public schools and the round blue bars in the toilets at all costs. In back of the Main House was an octagonal building that was our library, also dedicated to some rich, forgotten alum.

A huge, new athletic complex sported a great basketball court, a huge weight room with luminous new equipment I could never imagine lifting, squash courts, and a wrestling room with big green mats with our school's Latin logo in the center. I suspected that logos in Latin meant you could charge more for tuition. At the far end, opposite the basketball courts, was an older hockey rink. The school had apparently been a hockey powerhouse for years. The hockey players at the school all seemed to be a little bigger and a little dumber than the rest of the students.

Down a path from the Main House, built into the side of a hill, was a huge structure of immense, obtuse brownstone with large, arched doorways and several medieval-like turrets shrouding its four floors. It was dark and heavy and by far the most interesting structure on campus. For obvious reasons, it was called the Fort. The Fort was the school's original building at the "new" site and was where we ate meals and had school dances. The boarders lived upstairs. Day students weren't ever allowed to go up there.

The playing fields were even more impressive than the buildings. A major league style baseball diamond complete with green infield grass mowed in perfect squares sat at the middle of the complex. There seemed countless other football, soccer, field hockey, softball, and lacrosse fields, and even a large pond used for a summer camp held on campus. Surrounding everything were acres and acres of woods. Big, thick, and old. These were the playing fields of the cross-country team. I would run my ass off mostly because I was afraid of getting lost within the great, unfamiliar forestry. Lifelong suburban boys aren't in love with the woods.

"Yo, old man," Shaky started the second week of practice yapping at our coach.

"Yo, young, fat, out-of-shape kid."

"Who you calling fat and outta shape?"

"My name is Mr. Garrity."

"Yo, Mr. Garrity."

"Yo, young, fat, out-of-shape kid."

Our group laughed. The coaches were also teachers. Mr. Garrity taught math. Apparently he'd been some sort of successful business guy who had gone through a midlife crisis, dumped his wife, married a younger woman who supposedly looked just like his first wife, and became a teacher. He was actually a pretty good guy.

"Cut the shit, man. You know my name."

"Indeed I do, Francis."

"You know I hate being called Francis. My brothers call me Shaky."

"Does that mean I am one of your brothers?"

"Hell no. You're a skinny white old man."

"Then I'll call you Francis."

Our pack giggled again, and this time Shaky did as well. It was the first time I had laughed at my new school. And Shaky, named for his substantial abdomen, in his own way knew it. The big white-toothed smile on his dark face was the ignition for the whole group, like a match to kindling. When he would begin his deep, belly-heaving cackle, we no longer had control. We had to laugh too.

I would get to know Shaky pretty well that year. They put us together in all the dumb classes with the rich kids, the diversity kids, the hockey players, and the one other kid off the wait list. Mr. Garrity would occasionally refer to Shaky as our Fat Jack Falstaff. I, of course, didn't know who that was. I thought of him as the Norm Peterson of our school.

3.

A few weeks into the semester, I met the first girl I would get to know at Pendy. In my cloistered life up to that point, I had never really had a girl for a friend before, so this would all be virgin territory for me. She was the manager of the cross-country team. Those who didn't like to compete in sports could become team managers. Managing our team was a pretty lame role. There was no equipment and no real keeping score. Mostly she just sat and read her books while we ran through the woods. I had never even heard her speak until she approached me the first time.

"I'm surprised you're running cross-country. You seem like a jock."

I couldn't believe she even knew who I was.

"Hardly."

"Didn't I see you playing basketball in the gym the other day before practice?"

"You were definitely the only one who noticed."

She had purple hair, more earrings than I could count, and talked with a slight slur.

"Do you have a pierced tongue?"

She stuck her tongue out at me. A big, silver ball stared back. She was a sophomore and plainly had no shortage of self-assurance.

"Isn't that kind of uncomfortable?" I asked.

"I kind of like it."

"How do you chew your food?"

"The same way you do." She'd heard these questions before.

"Your parents don't give you a hard time?"

She just laughed.

"What's so funny?"

"I'll tell you someday when you know me better."

"It's your call."

The purple hair on one side of her head was quite a bit longer than the purple hair on the other side of her head.

"You like the hair?"

"I'm still trying to figure it out."

She laughed again. It was a nice laugh.

"I know," I said. "You'll tell me about it someday when I know you better."

"You don't talk like a jock."

"It's not clear that I am a jock."

"I told you. I saw you play basketball—and you looked like you knew what you were doing. You're a jock."

"How did you remember seeing me play basketball? I usually just shoot by myself."

The time I spent shooting baskets in the gym before cross-country practice was the only time during the school day I actually enjoyed. I wasn't confused by the rules, and I didn't have to talk to anyone. The sound of squeaking sneakers on the wooden floor was one of the few familiar sounds to me at this place. I would have stayed in the gym by myself all afternoon every day if they didn't make me do this ridiculous excuse for a sport.

"I always remember the cute ones."

I'm sure that I turned an eye-catching crimson tone. Only my grandmother and my Aunt Brook, who had never been married and probably never would, had ever called me cute.

"You're speechless." She continued to have her way with me. "Aren't you?"

Unlike those great scenes in television shows, I couldn't think of anything clever to respond. A half an hour from now, after I had the time to revisit the conversation in my mind a few times, I would be a stand-up comedian. Unfortunately, I would never have my own television sitcom.

"So how come you just manage the team instead of playing a sport?"

"I don't like to sweat."

"Well, there's no risk of breaking a sweat managing this team."

"Exactly."

"Have you ever played a sport?"

"Nope."

"Too bad."

"Why is that?"

"It's fun."

"You have fun running cross-country?"

"Cross-country isn't a sport."

"So why are you on the team?"

"I wish I knew."

"But you seem to run pretty well."

"There isn't a lot of skill involved."

I was definitely setting a personal record for my longest conversation ever with a girl. She was certainly a little off-kilter, but up to now I didn't have much experience to fall back on. Plus it's hard to be nervous when talking to someone with purple hair and a pierced tongue.

"You're new, aren't you?"

"Uh huh."

"How do you like it so far?"

"Not so much. It's a little overwhelming."

"You'll get used to it. Just takes a little time."

"I hope you're right. But I kind of doubt it."

"Don't be such a pessimist. You are going to be here for a long time."

"That's what I'm afraid of."

"Okay, so let's try to cheer you up. What are you doing this weekend?" she asked.

"I dunno."

I knew exactly what I would be doing this weekend. The same thing that I had done each weekend since school had started. I would sit in front of my new laptop all day on Saturday, pretending to do work and sneaking in as much *espn.com* or *Madden NFL* as I could. Every time I came up for air my father would grill me to see if I was studying hard enough—which I clearly wouldn't be. But in my mind I would be studying *long* enough. I'd watch television all Saturday night until I couldn't see anymore, and then I'd get up on Sunday, go to church with my family, and do the same thing all over again.

"You want to do 'I dunno' together?"

"Huh?"

"Do you want to do something?"

"Where do you live?"

"Cambridge."

Cambridge was on the other side of the river from Boston, where Harvard and unemployed street performers shared space. I'd been there only a couple of times before. Unremarkable suburban kids don't get to spend much time in Cambridge.

"How would I get there?"

"I'll come pick you up."

"How?"

"There is this great new invention. It's called a car."

"You drive?"

"All by myself."

"Sorry. I forgot you were older than me."

"Always will be."

"Okay."

"Okay what?"

"Okay. I'll go do something with you."

"Good."

"What's your name?"

"Jelly."

"Like the opposite of peanut butter?"

"It's short for Angela."

4.

There are no big yellow school buses at private schools. We came from too many different towns. Most of the older kids had their own cars. In fact, the student parking lot at Pendy looked a lot like a luxury car dealership—Lexus SUVs, BMW sports cars, VW convertibles. One senior had a Hummer. Except for Mr. Garrity, the entrepreneur-turned-math teacher, the cars of the faculty weren't even in the same league. The kids who didn't have driver's licenses usually carpooled until they were old enough to drive and get their own nice cars. I'd gotten into school too late to arrange for a carpool, so my mom dropped me off in the morning, and my dad—unless he was traveling, which was fairly often—picked me up on his way home in the evening after cross-country.

"Hey, Will."

"Hi, Pop."

"Sorry I'm late. Got caught up at work a little longer than I thought."

"That's okay."

"How was your day?"

"Good."

"What'd you do?"

"Nothing much."

"Anything interesting happen in assembly?"

"Nope."

"Classes interesting?"

"Not really."

"Lunch?"

"Had it."

"Anything good?"

"Never is."

"Would you prefer that I talk to the door knob?"

Fair point.

"I hear you. I'll try to be a better *raconteur*."

"SAT word?"

"Not bad, huh?"

My mom may have been the world's nicest person. When she picked me up after school, on the days my dad was traveling, we never talked about anything important. She was pretty for a middle-aged woman, and she had a pretty personality. Plus she really didn't care too much about my grades or where I was going to college. I mean, she cared, but it wasn't all consuming for her. More than anything else, she just didn't want any angst in our home. I loved those conversations in the car with her. Just she and I. My dad, on

the other hand, was becoming kind of a hardass. Since I'd gotten
into Pendy our relationship had begun to change. I mean, he loved
me and all that. But if we had been the same age, I doubt we would
have been friends. He was just way more driven that I was. He used
to tell everyone that his favorite part of the day was picking me up
at school. It was my least favorite part of the day. Because we had
cross-country practice after school, I didn't get picked up until
about six o'clock, which pretty much coincided with his schedule at
work. Since it seemed important to him, I tried my best to make it a
pleasant dialogue, although most times that was not easy. Invariably
during each drive home the conversation would lead to him lecturing
me on how I needed to work harder on my schoolwork. Given that
the previous year I'd worked only about a half an hour a night, I
thought I was stepping it up okay. But I knew whatever I did would
never be enough for him. We just had different expectations.

"Lot of homework?"

"Kind of."

"Can you handle it?"

"Yup."

"How are you doing in your classes?"

Dad, it's been only three weeks.

"Fine, I guess."

"Are you participating in class?"

"Yup."

"A lot?"

"Depends how much is 'a lot.'"

"Class participation is important in high school."

"I know, Dad."

"Just do your best."

No Dad, I'm going to try to flunk out.

"Yup."

So each night when I got home, I'd wolf down some food and head for my room and my new laptop. For the first half hour or so, I would just watch my two goldfish. We had gotten them in fifth grade for a science project. All of the other kids' fish died in a couple of weeks. Mine were still going strong, even though I didn't clean the little rectangle glass tank as often as I should have and the water would get pretty grimy. Plus I often forgot to feed them. But they were survivors. I had named one of the fish Lebron and the other Kobe. Kobe was the smaller, faster swimming fish.

Every half hour, I would take a break. My first break would be for a snack; I was always starving at night. I'd eat pretty much anything that had salt or sugar. During my second break, I would spend twenty minutes checking the glossy printed facebook the school gave to each student at the start of each year. I would try to memorize a couple of pages each night, looking at the pictures and addresses. The divorces were easy to tell. Parents with different last names and different addresses. The rich kids had their own phone numbers, separate from the parents. Some kids just had rich names. David Weston-Turner. Nathaniel Franklin Whitehouse III. Anyone named Nathaniel couldn't be hurting. Hartford was in that group. Kids of middle management were never named after a city. There were the required diversity kids from Boston. Like Shaky, a number of them had only one guardian listed and seemingly misspelled first names I'd had never heard before. My picture and information looked unbelievably generic.

"And promise me that you will work as hard as you can."

"Yup."

"I'm serious."

"Me too."

"Promise?"

"Uh huh."

"Scout's honor?"

"I was never a scout."

I could be a wiseass sometimes.

"How was cross-country?"

"It sucked."

"Will, you know I prefer that you don't talk like that."

"I know, but it still sucked."

"Did you run well?"

"I suppose."

"You suppose?"

"It's not even a sport, Dad. I'm just going to use it to get in shape for basketball."

When I was bored with my homework, I had begun to make a list in my notebook of ways to get kicked out of school. Not that I was serious, but it was an entertaining diversion. At first the list was basic—stuff that had been done many times long before I reached high school. But each night I would try to advance my idea from the previous night's drill. I thought I became quite creative over time.

1. Plagiarizing a paper
2. Drinking at a dance

3. Drinking during school
4. Drinking during lunch
5. Drugs (any kind)
6. Streaking across the field in the middle of a football game

I wasn't wild about the last one since I hadn't been through puberty yet. The whole show for the fans might have been a little embarrassing for me since there wasn't much to see.

7. Standing up during assembly and waving to Mr. Sanders, the headmaster
8. Standing up during assembly and singing our rival's school song
9. Sitting in one of the faculty chairs on stage during assembly
10. Get caught having sex with another student

Another problem one in that I didn't know how to have sex yet.

11. Get caught having sex with a teacher

Ditto.

12. Wear a scarlet "A" on my shirt but not get caught having sex with a teacher

The first book we read in English was *The Scarlet Letter*, so I felt this was a natural.

13. Starting a campaign to unionize the students

Civics class.

14. Starting a club for students to boycott homework

15. Writing a newsletter that made fun of the various faculty members
16. Pantsing Mr. Sanders during assembly
17. Pantsing Mrs. Sanders during assembly
18. E-mailing this list to the faculty

If anyone had ever seen my list, there was a reasonable chance that someone would legitimately argue I needed counseling. But that was part of being a kid. Much to my parents' chagrin I got to daydream. Only five hundred eighty-three nights of homework left.

And so after sufficiently screwing around for a couple of hours, I would finally get down to my serious homework.

> Write three pages, singled spaced, of critical analysis on the following question. Be sure to quote passages from the book to support your thesis.

> Statement: "Once I falsely hoped to meet with beings, who, pardoning my outward form, would love me for the excellent qualities which I was capable of bringing forth. I was nourished with high thoughts of honour and devotion. But now vice has degraded me beneath the meanest animal … the fallen angel becomes a malignant devil … I am quite alone."

We were reading *Frankenstein* in English class. It actually wasn't a bad book. This scientist, Victor Frankenstein, created in his laboratory a hideous monster. In its search for friendship the monster so scared the community that it ended up murdering those people with whom it should have been closest. The book was certainly better than the poetry that we had read in eighth grade. I hated poetry. Just because something rhymed didn't make it great literature. And if a poem didn't rhyme, it was just stupid.

> Question: What was the author's purpose in permitting the Monster to recount this last statement of remorse—his final confession—before taking his own life?

But this was the sort of thing I had a problem with in school. *Frankenstein* had been written a hundred and fifty years ago. *How the hell did I know what the author's purpose was?* I couldn't read the writer's mind—and Mrs. Sanborn, my teacher, certainly couldn't either. She may have been far more literary than I was, but these discussions were so dubious. She didn't know what the author, Mary Shelley, was thinking any more than I did. It was academic arrogance for her to think that she did. Hell, Mary Shelley was writing a story—and it was a pretty good story. She was probably just trying to make a few dollars to live on. This "critical analysis" stuff was crap. Why couldn't we just enjoy the story? Even though the paper wasn't due for a few days, I had no idea how the hell I was going to write three pages on this.

"Hey, Dad, you got a minute? I think I may need some help."

While he had been the source of most of the anxiety in my brief life, deep down my father was actually a decent person. I mean, he loved sports like I did. He coached me a lot, and he knew more than most of the coaches. We'd rarely take vacations so as not to miss any games, which I didn't mind at all. Because of him I was a smarter player than most kids my age.

He'd met my mother when they first got out of college and were working in Chicago. His job had brought them to Boston. I was born when they lived in the city, in a rented apartment in a brownstone in the Beacon Hill section of Boston. They had taken me there a bunch of times. When I was a few months old, we moved to the suburb of Wellesley. A few years later, my first brother came along, and then eventually a second.

The hard part of our relationship was that my father increasingly began to ride me all the time. He typically wouldn't yell; instead, he'd just needle me until I felt like throwing up. I dreaded when he would come into my room at night while I was pretending to work. He wouldn't say anything, but would steal a glance to see if I had been playing a game on the computer or reading *Sports Illustrated*, both of which I was usually doing, but I got better at hiding my misdeeds over time. It would drive him crazy if I was ever doing anything at home besides studying.

School just wasn't something I got excited about. I was pretty sure my feelings wouldn't ever change. But that's a hard message to deliver to your parents. And even if I had, it wouldn't have changed anything except that they would have kept tighter watch over me. So instead I just did my work to a level I surmised would let me get by. The rest of the time I worked on growing up bit by bit.

Unfortunately, the grading at Pendy was way harder than I was used to. Even getting a "B" was tough. On my first page English paper, I got a "See Me" for a grade. Mrs. Sanborn had taken a red felt pen and crossed out *every single line* in my paper. Even though my father asked me every night when he picked me up if I had gotten any papers or tests back that day, I never told him about that one. When I went to see her a few days later, Mrs. Sanborn told me I would have to put in extra time in order to catch up with the other kids. She said that I wrote at a sixth grade level. I figured that I had never been the greatest of writers, but it had seemed to be fine at my previous school. Somehow I lost a couple of years since entering high school.

"What do you need, Will?"

"Did you ever read *Frankenstein*?"

"A long, long time ago. Why?"

"I have to write a paper on it for English. I just don't really understand what the teacher is asking us to do."

My dad grabbed the assignment paper I handed him.

"Hmm. How about you give me a day to brush up on the book, and we can tackle this thing together this weekend?"

"That would be great, Dad."

The reality was that my father was thrilled when I asked him for help. It was his way of keeping tabs on what I was doing in school—and of making sure that I would get a good grade. I figured that if I kept my grades in the "B" range, I would be fine. My folks wouldn't be happy, but I figured that would be the right trade-off for the work I would otherwise have to put in. I also knew my father would find a way to read the whole book in a day and end up doing a really good job on this essay, which would help get my grade back into the range I needed.

The funny thing was that there were other kids who seemed to struggle academically way more than I did even though I was the kid who had gotten in off the wait list.

"Will, the phone's for you."

"Hello."

"Will?"

"Mmm."

"It's Hartford."

"Hey, Hartford."

"Have you finished your civics paper?"

"Yeah. It's due tomorrow."

"I know. Can I borrow it?"

"Borrow what?"

"Your civics paper."

"Huh?"

"I'm a little behind."

"Isn't that cheating?"

"It's not a big deal. I just need to get some ideas."

"Are you sure?"

"Yeah, I've done it before. I'm kind of a procrastinator. It helps unclog the brain cells, and then I can crank something out."

"I always thought you were one of the smart ones."

"It's only important they keep thinking that."

"I guess it's okay then."

"I owe you one, man. Can you just e-mail it me?"

"Mmm."

Apparently different kids had different strategies for getting their homework done.

5.

I WAS BOTH NERVOUS and kind of excited for my date with Jelly. I had been thinking about it since she first asked me out. This was new territory for me, and I had modest expectations. But since she had asked me, there wasn't as much anxiety involved. I wasn't really sure what to wear, but besides the clothes I wore to school and church, pretty much all I had left were t-shirts and jeans. So I put on a clean t-shirt, my semi-clean jeans and sort of combed my hair—something I did only on rare occasions.

My parents were going out to dinner with friends. And while they wanted to stay to meet my date, I convinced them to wait until next time. I knew if they saw Jelly with the purple hair and the pierced tongue there wasn't likely to be a next time.

"Thanks for picking me up."

"It might have been hard if I didn't," Jelly said, laughing at me. "You don't have your driver's license yet."

"I guess that's right."

"How long?"

"How long what?" I blushed.

"How long till you get your driver's license?"

"I dunno. Maybe a couple of years. I'm still only fourteen."

"Fourteen. Man, I really picked a young one."

"You want me to go back inside?"

"Of course not. You're still cute. How come they didn't redshirt you? I thought they redshirt all of the jocks."

"They probably didn't think of me as a jock. I'm only five foot four you know."

"Ah. But I see great promise."

"I'm glad somebody does."

I got into her car. It was a little red Honda Civic. Most of the rich kids had more expensive cars. She was a little harder to figure out.

"How come you didn't introduce me to your parents?"

"You wouldn't want to meet them."

"How come?"

"They'd just grill you about how much time you spend on your homework and what extracurricular activities you do. Then they'd beat on me when I got home for not doing as much as you."

"I bet you're exaggerating."

"I'll introduce you next time. Then you can judge for yourself."

"How do you know there is going to be a next time?"

Shit. My first date, and I'd already blown it.

"I really don't, I guess."

"Well, we'll just have to see if you behave yourself."

"I'll try."

"You are *sooo* very cute."

"You have to stop saying that."

"How come?"

"Because you sound like my grandmother."

"Does your grandmother have purple hair?"

"No. Hers is blue."

Jelly's car was more than a little messy. In fact, it was pretty much of a disaster—well below my admittedly low standards. Every surface was piled high with crap. All sorts of crap—sneakers, clothes, books, magazines, food wrappers. And it actually didn't smell that great. There was even an errant bra on top of black dress rolled up in the back seat. I probably stared a little too long, but except for my mother's and in the stores I'd never seen a real live bra up close and personal before. It was black and kind of small, but memorable nonetheless.

"So where do you want to go?"

"I dunno. You asked me out, remember?"

"I guess I did." She had a nice little giggle. "I guess you're too young to take to a bar."

"You go to bars?"

"Sometimes."

"How do you get in?"

"I have a fake ID."

"I wouldn't even know how to get one of those."

"You can buy them on Craigslist."

"Do you get drunk?"

"No. But I usually have a drink or two."

"Really?"

"Why so surprised?"

"I've actually never had a drink."

"Have you ever been on a date before?"

A date? I never even talk to girls!

"Does my cousin Molly count?"

"No."

"Then this is my first."

The girl with the purple hair just laughed and laughed.

"Hey," I was trying to keep from drowning, "I have to start somewhere, don't I?"

She just laughed some more.

"Is my boring social life that funny?" I asked.

"In a way, sort of."

"How so?"

"I'm gay. You picked a lesbian for your first date."

I was dumbfounded, a word my mother used a lot. For the first time in my life it had somehow seemed appropriate to the moment.

I mean, I kind of liked Jelly. She was entertaining in a different sort of way. But I don't think I'd ever even met a lesbian who was my age before. At least I was never conscious of having met one.

"You're a lesbian?"

"Yup."

"But how come you asked me out?"

"I just wanted to do something with you. Go out and have some fun. I didn't ask you to marry me, for God's sake!"

We rode in silence for a while as I sorted the news. Her driving skills matched her neatness.

"So do you have a girlfriend?"

"Kind of."

"What does that mean?"

"Well, I was seeing a girl over the summer, but she moved to Indianapolis. So I don't really get to see her anymore. We talk on the phone and text, but it's not the same."

"But you liked her?"

"That *is* why we saw each other."

"And so you got bored, had nothing to do, and so you asked me out."

"Basically."

"Man, you are really giving my ego a boost."

"But I've always thought you were cute."

"That doesn't really count, does it?"

"Why not?"

"Cause you don't like guys!"

"Details."

She was different. Certainly way different from anyone I had met before in my basically sheltered life. She was easy to talk to, and she was open. Most kids I knew never talked about anything seriously or honestly.

"I was worried I might have to kiss you goodnight. I guess now we can just shake hands."

"Man, guys are really strange."

"Probably can't argue with that."

My first date. Maybe I'd laugh about it someday, but at the moment I wasn't really seeing the humor. It seemed I was always a few steps behind.

"So how about we go play miniature golf? You don't need a fake ID for that."

"And no goodnight kisses are required."

6.

As the semester moved on, morning assembly became one of the better parts of my day. Despite being tired and hungry each morning, I actually started to look forward to assembly. Besides seeing Jelly in the hallways and shooting baskets in the gym before practice, it was the only part of the actual school day I could actually say that about. It was great people watching. Whether it was teachers or kids, you could always tell who liked who. Those who had romantic interests came to school each morning with a whole different energy—a sort of hormonal fission. The more they interacted, the more energy they created. Those who had no overlapping romantic interests, who were few, pretended they were doing some last minute studying, but were really hoping that someone would come up and share some of that fission with them. Each new morning there was renewed hope. It set the whole tone of the day for everyone. The first ten minutes of school could dictate whether it was going to be a good one or a bad one.

We sat in our assigned seats during assembly each morning. Assuming we didn't get kicked out, these would be our seats for the remaining four years of high school. On my left was Dawson the Claw from my cross-country team. On my right was Abby the Swimmer. They were my two constants each day. Next to those two I was actually an icon of stability.

Dawson never spoke. He'd come in each morning, always the first one there. He must have gotten up much earlier than I did as his pure blond hair was always perfectly combed, and his shirts never had the wrinkles that mine did. His thoroughness was almost girl-like. He was one of the few kids about my size, but for some reason I felt much bigger. I'd always say hi, but he only nodded and squeaked when I arrived and never made eye contact. I'd look right at him, but he would look at his shoes or my shoes or over my shoulder. We weren't in any of the same classes, and while he was certainly more than a little awkward, I got the sense he was pretty bright.

The skinny in school was that his father was the head of some big corporation and that they were filthy rich, flying their own jet all around the world for either business trips or vacations. But there were other kids in the school in the same boat. In fact, there were more of the super wealthy kids than there were of me. I'm sure the big price tag caused many people to self-select out of the Pendy admissions process. I'd also heard that Dawson's family was strict, by-the-book Mormon. No alcohol, no caffeine, no cursing. But since I'd seen him only nod and heard him only squeak, I really didn't know for sure.

Abby made up for Dawson's quiet demeanor. She arrived at school talking, and when she left at the end of the day she was still mid-sentence. I got to know a lot about her because she told me whether I wanted to hear it or not. Her father had dumped her mother for a news reporter from the local affiliate of one of the big television networks. Her mom had sort of melted down after that and seemed to be kind of out of the picture. She had a younger brother who was a basketball stud. I had seen him play, and he was really good. Her dad had built a half basketball court for her brother inside his house. From Abby's point of view, her father spent all his time working to build the brother's budding athletic career. She apparently was a terrific swimmer, but was left to raise herself in a big mansion and figure out what she wanted to do with her life. And based on her daily commentary, this seemed to change every day. So mostly I just listened and watched everyone else give off energy.

Maybe that's why I liked hanging out with Shaky on campus. His life was not one of privilege. Pendy actually was his only privilege. But he was straightforward and easy to read. He had no secrets that he wasn't willing to share with me. And maybe since I was such a simple person, I appealed to him as well. He probably understood my life a little more easily than those of kids like Dawson and Abby.

Since he and I were in all the same classes, we ate lunch together most days. Shaky could eat more than any person I had ever seen. He didn't care what it was—hamburgers, pasta, fries, bread, fruit—he would inhale it. Even if it wasn't on his tray, it was still fair game. Sometimes he'd use utensils, sometimes he wouldn't. It was as if whatever was in front of him was the only meal he'd have that day. But on a full stomach, he was usually in a good mood.

"So you wanna see my favorite place on campus?"

"I take it it's not the library."

"Shit no, man. I hate that place. Too many smart people. I gots ta have my freedom."

"Do I have a choice?"

We were coming out of lunch in the Fort. It was still one of those pretty nice fall days in New England. No need yet for a sweatshirt or jacket. We'd just eaten, and Shaky, per usual, had a pretty good haul. But we still had time to kill before the next period.

"You gots ta keep it a secret."

"I never really talk to anyone except for you and Jelly, so that's a pretty good bet."

"What's the deal with you and her anyway?"

"You got me."

"You like her?"

"She's a lesbian."

"I think she's hot."

"You going to change her?"

"I'd sure like ta try."

"So let's switch the subject. Where's this special place?"

"Up there."

Shaky pointed straight up. He was pointing to a turret, with a sliver of a window, above the top floor of the Fort.

"What's up there?"

"I told you. My special place."

"In the turret?"

"If that's what you call it."

"So what do you do up there?"

"Get away. Think. Take a nap."

"How do you get up there?"

"Come on. I'll show you."

We jogged out the front path that led to the Fort and slid around the corner to where the deliveries were made to the kitchen. The delivery dock, because it was the one unattractive part of the building, was largely hidden by strategically planted shrubbery. I had never been in this corner of the building before. Next to the delivery dock was a rusted, brown, padlocked door.

"It's locked."

"Yup."

Shaky proceeded to pull out the padlock hitch, which had been bolted to the mortar between the huge brown stones.

"The cement's worn away, so the metal latch pulls out. You can open the door without openin' the old lock."

From the look of the rusty padlock, it had not been opened in years.

"How did you figure this out?"

"You develop a sixth sense for things like this when you live in the projects. We always looking for places ta hide."

"So what's inside?"

"C'mon. I'll show you," he instructed.

We slipped inside into a dark, dusty room, and Shaky quickly closed the door behind us. I couldn't see anything.

"Follow me."

"How can I follow you? I can't see you. You're black, remember?"

"How could I forget? Follow ma voice. There's a set a stairs over to the right, up 'gainst the wall. Fin' the wall wit' your hand and then follow it."

I did as Shaky had instructed, following his grunting until I almost killed myself when my foot hit the base of the first step and I fell over, whacking the shit out of my shin.

"Shit!"

"Shhhh. Keep it down till we get ta our destination."

"Where're we going?"

"Up."

"How far?"

"Four floors. You'll be able ta see better as you get up. There's a window in the turret. You can see all the way ta Boston from up there. It's awesome, 'specially at night."

"You come up here at night?" I whispered because I was afraid of getting caught, but I whispered as loud as I could because I was more afraid that he would leave me alone in the dark.

"A couple 'a times."

We ascended the steps slowly—Shaky because he was grossly out of shape, and me because I couldn't see anything. It was bone dry and so dusty that it tickled my nose, but heeding his warning to stay quiet, I stifled any urge to sneeze. Since I had a free period after lunch, I wasn't worried about being late for anything. Plus anything that replaced time I should have been studying was fine with me.

"What floor are we on now?"

"Third."

"What's that?" I whispered at the top of my lungs.

I could make out the faint outline of a door.

"It's a door that goes inta the back of the janitor's closet on the third floor. You can get into the girl's floor through it."

The boy boarders supposedly lived on the second floor of the Fort, and the girl boarders supposedly lived on the third. Each floor had apartments on both ends of the hallways where married faculty couples resided. While day students were not allowed on the Fort's residential floors, I suspect that some had found ways to sneak in at some point during their time at the school. I had not done anything so venturesome up until this point.

"Have you done that?"

"One night late I was messing around. Walked the whole floor and peeked in on some of the girls without anyone knowing. Jessie Grabow sleeps wit' shit all over her face."

"You are unbelievable."

"One more flight 'a stairs."

We marginally picked up the pace on the final stretch of steps until we reached the zenith, and instantly I knew what he was talking about. The attic was big and parched, with stacks and stacks of old newspapers. The same grand brownstones we saw on the outside of the Fort stood guard up this high as the inside walls as well. I could only imagine the effort it must have taken to hoist these enormous stones into place four stories above the ground. It was evident that save for Shaky and me no one had been up in the turret in years. A few old metal milk crates were spread about the room to serve as seats when they were placed upside down. On the far side, in the middle of the curved wall, was a tall, thin window. You could see Boston.

The single window up so high let in enough light so that we could actually see. I pulled a newspaper off the top stack. *The New York Times*, July 7, 1967.

"Man, this was before I was born."

"Yeah, I done read that one. It's a good one. The Red Sox made it ta the World Series that year."

"You read it?"

"Yeah. It's fun. It's like visiting back it time. But you can do it on your own terms. It's like history class but wit' no homework and no tests. I can just absorb it 'cause I want to."

"I know what you mean."

The stacks were as high as I was. I counted sixteen piles in all. It was as if it was an old storage room that time had forgotten. I pulled a paper from another stack.

"Terrorists attack the Summer Olympics, killing two Israeli athletes and taking nine others hostage. That was September 5, 1972," I started to read.

"See. I had never heard 'a that. Again, long before your and ma time. But that stuff is interesting."

"August 9, 1974. Richard Nixon resigns."

"He was a old president, right?"

"We studied him last year in school," I commented. "He resigned before they impeached him."

"Meaning he was gonna get kicked out?"

"Yeah."

"I hope I don't get impeached from here."

"I wouldn't mind it so much. I mean, my parents would kill me, but I don't really like it here."

"Are you kidding me?"

"Why? You like it?"

"Beats getting shot at where I come from."

"That bad?"

"It's pretty bad."

I sat on one of the milk crates scanning my fourth old newspaper. Shaky sat on another, looking at nothing in particular.

"So what's it like to be rich?" he asked with no lead-in.

"I don't think I'm that rich."

"Your parents pay for this school, don't they?"

"Yeah, I guess."

"Thirty thousand big ones a year. A hundred plus thousan' by the time you graduate."

"Mmm."

"Then you rich."

"I guess I can't argue with that."

"So what's it like?"

"I can't say that I've ever thought about it."

"You have your own bedroom?"

"Yeah. Don't you?"

"I sleep on the couch 'a the living room in our one bedroom apartment."

"You live in an apartment?"

"Ain't too many houses where I live."

"You got brothers or sisters?"

"Nope. Just me and my grandma."

I truly had never thought of our family as being rich, but sleeping on the living room couch of a one bedroom apartment was a world apart from mine.

"Where do you do your homework?"

"At the kitchen table while my grandma watches TV at night. The school gave us a computer that we hooked up in the kitchen. We had ta bring it in early one Saturday morning b'fore everyone in the building was awake. Don't want no one ta know we have it. Else they might steal it."

"You're kidding, aren't you?"

"Never been more serious."

"How many apartments in your building?"

"Lots. Not sure exactly how many."

"Where is it exactly?"

"Dorchester. Ever been there?"

"I don't think so."

"You'd hate it."

"How come?"

"Everbody's black. It's poor, and there's more 'n' enough violence going around."

"You ever seen anyone killed?"

"Just my parents."

"Serious?"

"Uh huh."

"I'm sorry. That must have been hard."

"They were dealing drugs. They deserved it."

No parents. A one bedroom apartment. Pendy was a million miles away from his world.

"How come you and your grandmother stay there?"

"Not sure. It's kinds of all we know. I guess we're accustomed ta it. Plus my grandma loves her church. She goes there most days to sing or to pray. It's the only safe place in the neighborhood. I just don't think anyone ever hears her prayers, though."

"You go too?"

"Only when she makes me."

"Now I can relate to that."

And so here Shaky and I sat in his oasis. It was probably just as nice as the apartment where he lived, and apparently a lot safer too. It was easy to understand why he liked it so much up here.

"Hey, you want ta see a picture of Roger Clemens in his rookie year?"

"I don't ever remember him being so skinny."

"Who's Patty Hearst? She's on the front page of a whole bunch of these papers."

7.

Each semester the school made us take an elective course. It was supposed to be something that broadened our minds. I took theater the first semester, and it really sucked. My parents had wanted me to try out for a lead role. There was no way that was going to happen. In their own way, they seemed to sometimes think that I was still in elementary school and that I could put on a costume, go up on stage, say a few lines, and everyone would think I was cute and applaud. But the kids at Pendy could really act. They had serious talent and really knew what they were doing. There wasn't a chance I was going to get up on a stage and embarrass myself in front of the school, so I just did what they called "tech." That meant that I helped build the sets.

It was a stupid job. We were the bottom of the food chain and treated as such by the teachers who directed the play and the kids who were actors. Four of us did tech, and the only one I knew was Dawson. I was careful not to use the same paintbrush he used. Even after the final performance they made us stay until midnight to tear down the set while the cast went to a party. Ultimately, I didn't care too much. It was better than studying.

"So, Dawson, how come you don't ever say much to me?"

We were painting a skyline as a backdrop for the stage. It was pretty boring, and I was getting tired of brushstroke after brushstroke of toothpaste blue. So I thought I would try to strike up a conversation with Dawson to help pass the time.

True to form, he didn't say anything for a while. So I just sat there with my bucket of toothpaste blue paint and kept slapping it on the particle board. After about five minutes, he created the first audible sounds I had ever heard from him.

"I get nervous talking to people."

It wasn't exactly a breakthrough, but we had another half hour to go before we could go home, and I was unbelievably uninterested in what I was doing.

"Hey, I'm not that scary. And I've seen you talk to Abby and some of the really good looking girls in our class. I figured maybe I'd done something to tick you off."

It wasn't typical for me to initiate a conversation with someone I didn't know. But with Dawson, I certainly felt like I was the stronger person. Not superior, but certainly stronger. He was so mouse-like whenever I was around him. He looked like a decent kid, but I just really didn't know him.

"No, it's not that. I'm just a little different from a lot of the guys here. My family is pretty religious, so I get up and go to church services every morning before school. My parents are pretty strict. I'm not an athlete. I have five older sisters, so girls are pretty easy for me to get along with. I just don't have a lot to say to guys."

"You have to go to church every morning?"

He could have told me he was a hit man for the Mafia but I wouldn't have heard it. I was stuck on his church attendance.

"Yeah."

"Do you like going?"

"I kind of do."

"Really?"

"I take it you don't."

"My family makes me go every Sunday, but I don't really believe in God."

"How come?"

"I don't know. I guess it's like Santa Claus coming down the chimney or the Easter Bunny and the eggs. All the stories never really seemed very realistic to me."

I had stopped painting and was just sitting on my stool. Dawson didn't stop and never once looked at me, though given our history I didn't expect him to. He just kept painting toothpaste blue.

"I believe in God."

"Really?"

"Yes."

"I have trouble because it isn't really tangible. How are we supposed to know if all that stuff ever really happened?"

"Does it make a difference whether it did or not?"

"Shouldn't it?"

"Learning about God is learning about goodness. Whether there was a Good Samaritan or a Wedding at Cana is irrelevant to me. What is relevant is that we understand the good that He stands for. Without God, who is there to remind us of our values and how we should treat each other?"

No doubt this was an interesting first conversation for Dawson and me. For whatever reason, I was determined to try to learn a little more about him. Whether he liked it or not, he was part of my daily landscape, so it seemed only fair.

"Do you read the Bible and pray and stuff like that?"

"Yes I do."

"And you like doing that?"

"I'd like to think that God understands me."

"Heck, I'm just trying to get my parents to understand me."

For the first time in the three months since we'd first started sitting next to each other in morning assembly, I actually saw Dawson smile.

"I know what that feels like. I do better with God than I do with my parents."

8.

At the start of November, we read a book in English class called *Twelve*. It was different from any book that I had ever read before. It was about purposeless, rich, prep school kids in Manhattan who were getting messed up on alcohol and drugs. Every page had a couple of swear words, and these kids, who were my own age, slept with anyone to get the newest designer drug. The writer was only twenty-one and had lived through it. Yet another world I knew nothing about.

I had heard plenty of talk at my new school about parties and getting drunk. Three juniors were suspended in November for being caught drinking in a car on campus. I hadn't really heard anything about drugs. But I had never witnessed students doing either. It could have been that I was very naïve. I wouldn't have doubted that. On the other hand, it could just have been that except for my one misguided date with Jelly, I never went out.

It was too much work.

I was pretty happy when November came and cross-country was over. It was a dumb sport, but I will admit that I was in great physical shape, better than I had even been in before. I was kind of proud of that. As the fall had progressed and the days had become shorter and shorter, I'd run my ass off to get out of the woods before darkness settled in. By the time the season ended, I was clearly the second best guy on the team. Not that anybody cared. It was only cross-country.

We had a week off between seasons, and I went to the gym every day after classes to shoot baskets. Most days I just shot by myself. A lot of the older kids would be playing pickup games, and a couple of times they needed another guy and asked me to play. But for the most part, I just shot alone.

The basketball court was my refuge. There was something about stepping onto the court. Sweaty t-shirts, squeaking sneakers, the occasional whistle. I was never happier than I was when I had a ball and a hoop. Everything was so clear on the court. I knew the game. I knew the rules. There were no gray areas. If the ball went in the bucket you got two points; if it didn't, you got zilch. And the score was final. There was no ambiguity. I didn't have to pretend that I knew what Mary Shelley was thinking.

"Will."

"Yes, Coach?"

"You've played very well in tryouts. You're a smart little player. I'm going to put you on the JV team and hope you grow."

Yes!

"Sounds good to me, Coach."

"I want you to play point guard. Think you can handle that?"

"Sure."

Yessss!

"I'm looking forward to good things from you."

I had been feeling like I needed to catch a break at this school, and maybe this was it. Most of the guys in my class played on what they called the thirds team. In public school they called it the freshmen team. The private schools even made the team names sound older and more of a tradition, certainly just another reason to charge higher tuition. Three freshmen made the JV. It felt good to be better than other kids at something.

"Hi, Pop."

He was on time picking me up.

"Hey, Will. You seem happy."

"I made the JV team."

"Really?"

"Uh huh."

"Way to go! I take it you played well?"

"I didn't think I shot that well. But my ball handling and defense were pretty good, and I hustled my butt off."

Sports were the primary area where my dad and I bonded. It always provided a common ground for us to talk. Through all the physical, social, and emotional ebbs and flows of teenage life, this was our constant. We spoke the same language and appreciated the same little triumphs. There was nothing that made him happier than when I played well. He could sense my happiness as I sat in the passenger seat of his car. It had been a while since I had experienced this feeling. It had a welcome familiarity.

"Can you keep up with the older kids on junior varsity?"

"Can't shave like they do. But I can play ball with them."

"Think you'll play much?"

"I think I may start. There's only one other point guard, and I'm better than he is."

"That's great, Will. I'm really happy for you."

"Yeah. Me too."

"I'll have to clear some time on my schedule to come see the games."

"That would be great."

"What days do you play?"

"Mostly Wednesdays and Saturdays, I think."

"You know, you're going to have to work a little smarter to keep your grades up. You won't have much free time anymore."

He couldn't even wait a minute.

9.

"How come you're eating lunch by yourself?"

"Dunno. Kind of just happened. I don't mind it. I really like this building. It's kind of fun to just sit here and look around."

"You're getting weird."

"Nah. Been that way forever."

Jelly looked good—and different—as always. She was a part of my regular routine, and I liked that. Because she was a year ahead of me, we weren't in any of the same classes. I got the sense that she was pretty smart. So even if we had been in the same grade, we probably wouldn't have been in the same classes. But occasionally we would cross paths during the day, which would make it a better day. She would usually blow me a kiss or some other out of the norm gesture, but that's what made her Jelly. I didn't embarrass as easily as when I first met her.

"Heard you made the basketball team."

"JV."

"Hey, that's still pretty good for a freshman."

"Yeah, I guess."

"Can I come to your games?"

"So you can embarrass me?"

"Of course."

"Have you ever been to a Pendy basketball game?"

"No."

"Have you ever been to a Pendy sporting contest of any kind?"

"Cross-country. Remember?"

"That's not a sport. Besides, all you did was read your books."

"I used to watch you run."

"Yeah, right."

"I did. Remember, I think you have that nice ass."

"You know, that may not be as great of a compliment as you think given that you prefer girls. I don't know about having my ass compared to some chick's."

"Jealous?"

"Probably a little."

I think one of the reasons that I had grown to like Jelly was that we could have such conversations. I talked increasingly openly and was less inhibited with her than I had been with anyone in my life. With anyone else—my teachers, my parents, classmates—I was measured in what I said. Not confident enough that anything I was doing or talking about was anything I should be that proud of. But in so many ways with Jelly it didn't matter.

"So can I ask you a question?" I continued.

"Sure, lovey."

"Are your parents straight or gay?"

"What brought on this new fascination with my family?"

"I don't know. I'm getting to know you better, and I was just thinking about it. I guess I was just curious."

"Well, one's skinny and one's fat. Like Laurel and Hardy. Including the mustache. But they're both lifelong lesbians. Came out of the closet when they were in junior high, long before it was a cool thing to do. Started dating in high school and have been together ever since."

"Were you adopted, or did they have you normally?"

"Normally?"

"You know what I mean."

"I usually do. That's why I like you so very much."

"Thanks. I think."

"They talked some friend of theirs into being the sperm donor. I guess I look like him."

"Have you ever seen him?"

"Nope."

"So you're a test-tube kid?"

"No. It was a one shot deal. One time is all it took. At least that's what they told me."

"Wow."

"Pretty weird, huh?"

"It's a long way from my family. We're more like a *Happy Days* rerun."

"Trust me. There are some advantages to that."

"I suppose." I thought for a while before I asked my next question. "Have you ever wanted to see the guy who contributed his sperm? I mean, are you curious at all?"

"Geez, this is kind of deep discussion for you, isn't it?"

"I've been known to have some depth to me on rare occasions. I just find the whole thing kind of interesting."

"Kind of interesting?"

"Well, something like that anyway. I guess it is all part of what makes you so different."

"So is it good different?"

"I guess so."

It was great different, but I wasn't yet prepared to show my feelings. I was beginning to crawl out of my shell, but mine was a big shell, and I was a slow crawler.

"So when are we going out on our second date? We can examine my life in more detail then if you're still interested."

"Your call. You have the car, remember? And yes, I'll still be interested."

"Can you fit it in your tight basketball schedule?"

"It may be tough, but I think I can make room for you. Besides, Christmas break begins in a few weeks. We don't have any basketball over vacation."

"Good. I'd like that."

"Hey, before you actually say anything else nice to me, I'd better get to class. Don't want to be late for Bussmann. He's my best grade—can't afford to lose my status."

"Isn't that incongruous? Bussmann, the dean of discipline, is your easiest teacher."

"Could be. But as usual I'm not exactly sure I know what that word means."

10.

"YO, WILLMAN."

I looked around to make sure that it was the biggest guy in school talking to me. Six foot eleven. Black. Cornrows dangling down to his shoulders, and the beginnings of a goatee on his chin. His teeth were more than a little crooked. Nonetheless, for someone of my stature, it was like talking to Zeus. This was the first time I had ever heard him speak. Zeus's voice was a little higher than I had expected.

"Yes, sir."

"Sir?"

"Sorry. I didn't know what to say. You never talked to me before."

"You know, dog, you go round calling people 'sir' and somebody's going to think you're a queer."

"I guess I can understand that."

"You're not a queer, are you?"

"No, I don't think so."

"So you want to play on my team?"

"For the three-on-three?"

"Yo. Got to have one girl and one kid not on the varsity."

"I would be the one kid not on varsity."

"Man, you ain't gonna be the girl, are you?"

"No, I guess not."

"I seen you play on JV. You're pretty good. All you got to do is pass the ball to me."

"I can do that."

"Figured you could."

"Who's the girl going to be?"

"Thought maybe you could help me with that. I don't know many of the girls here."

That made two of us.

"Sure. I'll find somebody if you want."

"Yeah, you do that. But make sure she's good. You know any girls who are good basketball players?"

"Not really. I only know about two girls in the whole school."

"Shit."

"But don't worry. I'll figure something out."

"You sure you can do it?"

"Hey, I want to be on your team. I'll ask every girl in school if I have to."

"Good, 'cause I wanna win. Last year I lost in the finals."

"I won't let you down."

"No shit."

When the best athlete in the school talks to a freshman, it feels pretty good. When he goes out of his way to ask you to be on his team for the annual school basketball contest that includes most of the boys, girls and faculty members in the school, it feels incredible.

I was beginning to build a little reputation for myself because of my basketball skills. In high school there were basically two ways to get a good reputation—either be cool or be a good athlete. My sense is that it had been that way since the beginning of time. I was never going to be cool, so basketball was all that I had going for me. I had scored seventeen points in the previous day's game and was on a high. Sometimes on the court you get into a zone while everybody else seems to be in slow motion, and the previous day had been one of those days. All my decisions and movements were just a little bit ahead of everyone else's. I don't know why this sense is there some games and not others, but it had been there the day before. I wished I could bottle that feeling of invincibility, not just on the court but everywhere in my life. The leather left my hand, and there was nothing but nylon. I had been good. Since basketball was really the only important thing in my life, I was in a great mood. And it was great that I'd been noticed by the best player in school.

For the three-on-three I figured I could always get Abby. She was pretty big, was athletic and had good basketball genes. She'd certainly be thrilled if I asked her. It would give her something to talk about for the rest of the year.

"Hi, Mr. Bussmann."

The big man was barreling down the hallway of the Main School, looking in no mood to be tangled with. One of his infamous Buzzsaw moods. I had never seen him lose his temper before, but the consensus was to steer clear when he got pissed off. His face was almost always red because he labored so hard with all the extra weight he carried. But when he was about to lose it, the red turned to purple. I figured I'd just offer my obligatory greeting and get out of his way. After all, he was my teacher, and I couldn't rudely ignore him.

I was stunned when he grabbed my shoulder and basically dragged my scrawny frame down the fifty feet of hallway to his tiny office in the center of the building. My shoulder was like a coat hanger in his thick, calloused hand. He wasn't hurting me at all, but I could see from the looks of the other kids in the corridor, who had turned stone silent, that this was going to be no joy ride.

"Sit down!"

Once inside his office, he essentially threw me into the wooden captain's chair facing his desk and slammed his door shut. It was the sole chair, other than his desk set, in a room crammed with folders, pads, magazines, old sweaters, and boots that made his already tiny, airless office a pothole. I had never been in the office before, nor never had really wanted to be. Bussmann was the dean of discipline; being in his room didn't have much upside. I had no idea why I was there, but I was scared shitless.

More than ever in my life.

"William!"

A dark purple vein—darker than his then purple face—was popping out of the middle of his forehead. It stretched from his hairline to the bridge of his nose. I couldn't look at anything else, hoping all along it wouldn't burst. Me and Buzzsaw and his big, purple vein together in his office. His entire oversized body was shaking from anger; my skinny little body was beginning to shake with fear.

"Yes, sir."

The purple vein throbbed and throbbed. It was like it was reaching out to tell me something, to warn of the terrific force of the Buzzsaw that was about to be laid upon me. I wished I could hear what it was saying.

"What the hell is the matter with you!"

He stood in front of me, as angry as I had ever seen anyone, and even though his voice had a bit of a smoker's hoarseness to it, I was sure that all of the kids up and down the Main School hallway were able to hear every word he was saying. I wondered how many had ever seen the throbbing little person sitting on his forehead, still trying its best to warn me.

"Mr. Bussmann?"

I thought he was going to kill me.

Then he held up a civics paper I had submitted many weeks ago. In huge red ink was written what no student ever wants to see—no matter how little effort he, on average, puts into his homework: *Plagiarized.*

Holy crap! How the hell did he even get my paper? I'd written it for Mr. Reese's civics class. Bussmann taught Math.

"I don't get it, Mr. Bussmann. I thought I actually did a pretty good job on that paper."

By my modest standards anyway.

"I expect Hartford thinks the same thing!"

Uh oh.

"Imagine Mr. Reese's and Mrs. White's reaction when they eventually realized they got the *exact* same paper submitted twice!"

"The exact same paper?"

The exact same paper?

My lower lip quivered, and my body shivered even more. As much as I wanted it to stop, I couldn't control it. I was sitting in this crappy, hot little office and freezing to death.

"Young man, I don't know what the protocol was at your previous school, but here we do our own work! I have never in my day seen anything so brazen or stupid."

"But, Mr. Bussmann, I *did* do my own work."

My voice sounded incredibly high—more like a young girl's.

"Like hell you did!"

The purple man on his forehead was now dancing. If it burst, I didn't know what I would do. I didn't know how to put a tourniquet on someone's head, and giving CPR to a teacher was not something high on my list—particularly one who smoked a lot. I did the only thing I could, given the situation, which was to begin to cry uncontrollably. I wasn't proud of it. I hadn't cried in a long time. But I couldn't help it.

"I didn't copy anyone's paper! I wrote it myself!"

"Call your parents and have them come get you."

"No!"

I wasn't in the habit of talking back to teachers, and I was deathly afraid of Buzzsaw, but I was more afraid of my father.

"What?"

My guess is that no one had talked back to him in a long, long time.

"You can't do this to me! I wrote that paper! I can prove it to you!"

"Your days are done here, young man."

I couldn't believe I was hearing him say this. I was finally getting a little rhythm in this school. Basketball was giving me a life. My relationship with Jelly was confusing but something I somehow enjoyed. Shaky and our oasis. Even Dawson and Abby. So I was finally beyond just treading water, and Buzzsaw was going to take it away. It just didn't seem fair.

At that point some force inside of me took over. I stood up from my chair to face Bussman, extended my small frame as tall as it would go, pulled my arm back and punched Bussmann right in the middle of his enormous midsection. Every last morsel of strength in my undersized little body went into that punch. I didn't know I had that kind of power in me.

Bussmann looked like he had swallowed a watermelon whole. He stumbled back into his desk chair, the wind gone from within him, his eyes showing nothing but disbelief. Disbelief that I had copied a paper word for word and handed it in as my own. Disbelief that I could pack such a punch. I was certain the purple vein was now ready to burst.

I ran from his office without stopping to see if he was all right. The kids in hallway, who had no doubt been listening to the screaming match, just stared as I sprinted by. I had no idea where I was going. Just like when I threw the punch, some uncontrollable inner force was guiding my actions.

I kept running for a long time, without regard to where I went or what I was going to do. The running was easy; I had been doing that all semester. But my mind was racing faster than my legs. It shouldn't have surprised me that I ultimately ended up amid the big, old trees that made up the cross-country course. While it was not my favorite place on campus, and I would always be afraid there after dark, it was the place I knew best. It was cold and wet in the woods. By the time I finally stopped running, my shirt was drenched with a combination of tears, sweat, and the previous night's cold rain dripping from the leaves of the trees. My basketball sneakers were also soaked and began to squish with each step I took. It wasn't yet lunchtime, yet I had no idea what to do.

And I just couldn't stop shivering.

II.

Hartford ultimately was expelled from the school, despite his father's pull. When the teachers started digging into it, they recognized it wasn't the first time he'd copied other people's work. Only this was the most bold. He was so lazy, he had just copied my paper verbatim and figured that no one in his or her right mind would take my word over his. Give him credit; he came close. It didn't matter much, though. I understand he was accepted at another good school and eased right back into being Hartford. He actually wasn't a bad kid; he just made some bad decisions.

I was wrong to have given Hartford my paper. But he had taken advantage of my naïveté. In my mind, his crime was for worse. What surprised me was that I seemed to care. Buzzsaw had threatened me with expulsion, and, without thinking, I fought back with every bit of strength I possessed. It was not planned. But it was an honest rebuke that I couldn't have controlled even if I'd wanted to. In my life up until then, I don't think I had ever pushed back that hard for anything.

So while I was pardoned for the cheating, there was still the issue of punching Mr. Bussmann that I had to deal with. On the whole, teachers don't much like being hit in the stomach—especially when the teacher was the dean of discipline.

"So how hard did you hit him?"

"Pretty hard, I think."

"He must have been freaked."

"I don't know. I didn't stick around to watch."

"What did you do?"

"I ran like hell."

"See. Cross-country training is becoming worthwhile for something."

"It's not that funny, Jelly. I was scared. In fact, I still kind of am."

"I think it's funny. You may be building a bit of a reputation here. The kid who smacked the dean of discipline."

"I think I'd rather go back to being invisible."

"What did you parents say?"

"Except for the hitting the teacher part, they were actually pretty good."

"What's the school going to do to you?"

"They haven't decided. I just hope they don't take basketball away."

"That would suck."

"You can say that again."

"That would suck."

Mr. Bussmann was reasonably understanding after our confrontation. He was probably never going to forgive me as I really had embarrassed him. No adult likes that. But he did actually apologize for losing his temper without knowing all the facts. I thought that was pretty honorable of him. I'm not sure many teachers would have done that. And since I still was going to have him as my teacher for the rest of the year, it helped ease what could have become an untenable relationship. My new, six foot eleven inch, cornrowed friend wasn't as understanding. He smelled trouble—like the risk of my getting expelled—and dumped me from his team for someone else.

I wished that I'd been more calm with the Bussmann situation. I think I could set world records for how quickly I'd unraveled under pressure. Always had. By high school I figured I wasn't supposed to cry anymore. But I had really been gushing in Buzzsaw's office. It's funny that I was so affected by the threat of being kicked out. Almost a full semester at Pendy, and I certainly didn't feel comfortable yet. Maybe subconsciously I didn't want to start over at a new high school. Or maybe I just didn't like controversy when I was at the center of it. Or perhaps I cared more about my reputation than I thought. That would represent new heights for me.

THERE IS NO WORSE time in life than waiting for report cards when you know your grades were going to suck. My goal had been to get a "B" average. I wasn't even going to be close. Mid-term exams had been harder than I had anticipated. All the fake studying I did hadn't prepared me. I bombed, and I knew it.

So instead of enjoying Christmas vacation, I just kind of sat around each day, cringing with the sound of the mail dropping through the slot in the front door. Each day there was no letter from Pendy was a reprieve for me. Finally, New Year's Eve came in with a bang.

"Will!"

"Yeah Dad."

"Front and center!"

Uh oh.

"What's up, Dad?"

I knew full well what was up. And it wasn't my grades.

"Have you seen your grades?"

"No."

"Well, would you like to see them?"

"I doubt it."

He handed me the printed page with the bold green Pendy logo across the top.

Math	B
English	C
Civics	C-
Biology	D+
Spanish	C-
Tech Theater	C

Math was pretty good, given what I had been through with punching Bussmann and all. Dad was going to kill me for the rest of them though. In days of serious competition for choice admissions spots to the best colleges, a "C" was like flunking.

"These are not very good grades, Will."

"I know, Dad."

"In fact they stink."

"I know."

"Every time I asked how you were doing in school, you always answered 'fine.'"

"I know."

"Are you over your head?"

"No. I can do the work."

"Then how the hell do you explain this?"

For as long as I can remember, when my dad got pissed at me I always responded in the same way. For the second time that semester I cried. I still wasn't proud of it, and I don't know if I did it on purpose, but it was sort of a natural reaction. And my dad hated when people cried. He didn't know how to respond. My mom always used that tactic quite effectively on him too.

13.

BEING THE FATHER OF *a teenager was more stressful than I had ever imagined, but not for any of the reasons I had expected.*

I had always told myself that keeping my son alive was my most important objective in parenting during his high school years. I'd watched as another couple in town lost their seventeen year old son the previous spring in a horrible car accident when he was driving drunk while trying to speed home by his curfew. A straight "A" student and an incredible baseball player, he was headed to Stanford the following fall but was too drunk to navigate a winding road on the way home from a party at a friend's house. The car skidded on a patch of black ice, and he landed fifty feet from the wreckage. He would have graduated in just three more months.

I read of six other high school kids that same spring and summer who had died in tragic, avoidable incidents in the towns surrounding mine. The invincibility of teenagers was, of course, a fallacy, but one that was so hard for them to comprehend. Until, of course, it was too late.

With Will, we hadn't had any of those issues, and I was reasonably comfortable that we wouldn't in the future. Though with the pending onset of puberty and a driver's license over the next year or two, it was hard to be certain. But the challenges with Will were much more basic.

Will was fundamentally a great kid. And being our first, we were certainly practicing on him. But he was, at the same time, confusing and frustrating. He lacked any initiative whatsoever and would have been happiest watching ESPN Sports Center or old television sitcom re-runs twenty-four hours a day. He regularly wasted ungodly amounts of time. With the exception of basketball, he didn't seem to care about anything.

So mostly I barked at him every chance I could. I didn't feel great about it. It certainly wasn't fun. And it was clear that it was placing a strain on our relationship. But I had the feeling that the only way that he was going to succeed in high school was for us to ride him. So for better or for worse, he was going to be in for quite a ride.

"You know, I'm going to have to ground you because of those grades."

"I know. But I never really go out anyway."

"I realize that, but I still have to ground you. It's what parents are supposed to do."

"Mmm."

Lifeless as always. Except when he cried, he never showed any real emotion. I couldn't understand why it was so hard to get through to him. I know as parents we always thought we had been more disciplined in our youth—working harder, studying more, etc. But in this case, there was no comparison. It wasn't even close. And man did I hate when he cried. He was too old for that kind of crap now.

"Don't you want to do well in school, Will?"

"Of course I do, Dad."

"Your effort doesn't reflect that desire."

"*I know. I was stupid. I'll get it right.*"

"*How can I be sure of that?*"

"*I can get it done.*"

"*Maybe I should spend more time with you on your studies.*"

"*Sure.*"

Per usual, he would say anything he thought would get me off of his back for the moment.

"*How about I sit in your room while you are studying? I have plenty of my own work to do at night. You can ask me questions if you need help. And it might help you build some studying discipline if you know that I am there all the time.*"

"*Whatever.*"

"*Will, I don't know that you have another choice.*"

"*I don't doubt that.*"

"*Good. We'll start tonight.*"

"*It's New Year's Eve.*"

"*You have some catching up to do.*"

"*Happy New Year, I guess.*"

My PARENTS COULDN'T DO anything to change my first term grades. So there were a lot of threats, deals, and bets, but I knew that they weren't going to pull me out of Pendy; it would have been too embarrassing for them. So second term came, and I was back to my usual uninspiring performance.

For the second semester, I signed up for photography as my elective. I really didn't know anything about it, having never picked up a camera in my life before. It fit my schedule, and there didn't seem to be any heavy lifting. And it had to be better than tech theater. I hated that. My parents bought me the three hundred dollar camera required for the course.

Incredibly, photography opened up a whole new world for me that I'd never known to exist. I got to do just what I like to do best, which was to watch but not participate. It was like a two-way mirror; I could see everything, but no one could see me. It was probably my first great intellectual revelation at Pendy.

"You actually have a nice touch, Will."

"Thanks, Miss Van Waters. You sound surprised."

"In fact I am."

"Me too."

Miss Van Waters was the first teacher at school I could joke around with. She was young, single and rumored to be pregnant. But I couldn't tell. She was pretty big to begin with. But she was always complimenting me on my work, which was far different from the feedback I got in my other classes. And different from home. I was not that dissimilar from everyone else. I liked accolades too.

"Are you sure you've never used a camera before?"

"Scout's honor. Never even a Polaroid. I'm a total rookie."

It was nice to be able to be completely honest with a teacher for once. And not to have to make any excuses.

"You don't take pictures like one. You have a good eye for catching situations most of us don't see."

"Really?"

"Yes. Take this one for example. A photograph of one of the maintenance workers taking a break and having a Coke and a cigarette. Tired and pensive. How many of us have even noticed these working guys around here? We're too busy with our own selfish pursuits. It reminds me a little bit of a famous series of close-ups taken of migrant farm workers in the Oklahoma Dust Bowl drought during the Depression. They were done by a woman named Dorothea Lange. Made her famous."

"Does this mean I'm going to be famous?"

"Well, maybe not just yet. Your pictures are still off center, and you are overexposing when you develop them. But you are off to a good start. Keep practicing, okay?"

"I can do that."

So I started toting my camera around during my free periods and snapping pictures. I usually couldn't wait to get to the dark room to develop them. Some days I would have fifty or sixty pictures to develop. Most of the time I was disappointed with the results. The picture in my mind and what came out on the chemical paper were not even similar. But every once in a while I nailed it. And when I got the picture right, there was no better feeling. I didn't need anybody else's confirmation. When I got it right, I just knew it.

"So do you make love to that camera of yours?"

"Huh?"

It was just before lunch, and I was sitting on a rock under a tree in the woods watching kids walk from the Main School to the Fort on their way to eat. Even when I was trying to hide, Jelly could find me. Not that I minded.

"You're always carrying that thing around now. You never talk to people. Instead you just hide in a corner and photograph them. It's a little creepy, you know."

"You should see my pictures. I'm actually getting pretty good."

"I took a tour of the art room yesterday."

"You don't take art."

"I wanted to see your stuff. I wanted to see what you notice when you're wandering around."

"Usually nothing very important."

"I looked through your portfolio."

"You did?"

"Of course."

"You're not supposed to look at our stuff!"

"I only looked at yours."

"Should I feel violated?"

"Hardly. It's actually really good."

"I suspect that I should say thank you, but I feel there is a catch."

"Naturally."

"Are you going to tell me?"

"There are no pictures of me in there."

"I know. I took the pictures, remember?"

"All your pictures are of people. None of the pictures is of a landscape or foliage—traditional stuff. But there must be pictures of at least two hundred people from this campus just in your portfolio. That doesn't count what's hanging on the wall or still in your camera."

"And that's a problem?"

"Yes."

"How come?"

"I already told you. There aren't any of me."

Jelly was right. I was surprised she actually cared.

"Believe it or not, I suspect there's a reason for that," I said.

"I'd break the camera lens?"

"Hardly."

"So what is it then?"

The reason was all too simple.

"I know you too well."

And maybe it would give me a little bit of an edge in our relationship for the first time.

"What difference does that make?"

"I take pictures of people I don't really know—which is pretty much everyone but you. I try to understand who they are through my lens. Try to catch them in a moment that others, including me, might not usually see. There is nothing a camera lens can show me about you that I don't already know."

"I bet you're wrong."

"I don't think so."

"Will you take my picture now?"

"Nope."

"But someday you will."

"I doubt it."

"Haven't you learned yet that you should never doubt me?"

"We'll see."

15.

ONE OF THE PROBLEMS with punching a teacher is that they begin to take a more earnest interest in your development. Even though Hartford received most of the blame, I knew I was still walking a tightrope. I knew if I ever came close to crossing the line with a teacher again I'd be following Hartford out the door.

So Buzzsaw made me do the spring play. He wasn't even involved in theater, but he found out in a teachers' meeting that the play needed another male actor—as far more girls had tried out than boys. So knowing he had the upper hand with me, he readily offered my services. I wanted to play baseball, but he wasn't going to give me the chance. And while my father would have preferred that I played a sport, he was happy that I hadn't been expelled for punching a teacher, so he wasn't going to cross Buzzsaw either. Jelly, of course, immediately found the humor in this.

"You're going to be in the spring play?"

"I wasn't really given a choice."

"I think this is really, really funny."

"Want to take my place?"

"And miss your performance? I'm planning on getting a front row seat."

"I have no idea how to act."

"Isn't the play called *Children of Eden*?"

"Yeah."

"Have you ever heard of it?"

"Of course not."

"How many other boys are in the play?"

"I'm not sure. But they needed another guy. That's why I got drafted."

"What role are you playing?"

"I guess I'm playing the father."

Jelly start to laugh. I usually liked her laugh. But this time it kind of haunted me.

"Is it that funny?" I asked. But she still kept laughing. Obviously laughing at me, not with me. Kind of like when I discovered on our date that she was a lesbian. "Did I miss something?"

"You sure did."

"What?"

"Do you know anything about the play?"

"Nope."

"*Children of Eden* is the story of creation. You know, as in the Bible—Adam and Eve, Cain and Abel. Remember all those stories from your Sunday school days? Kids from *Happy Days* reruns always go to Sunday school, don't they?"

"Yeah, I remember some of that stuff."

"So you play Father?"

"That's what they told me. I'm playing the father."

"You are missing the whole thing here. You are not playing 'the father.' You're playing Father. With a capital F."

"Is this a word game you're playing with me?"

"You're playing God."

Now that would be interesting.

I had to stop and think about that for a minute. I had all sorts of thoughts on this one—from my conversations with Dawson to the fact that I didn't believe in God.

"You don't think I can play God?"

"It's a lead role. There are going to be lot of lines to memorize."

"Yeah, that's going to be a problem."

Jelly continued her haunting laugh.

"That's the least of your worries?"

"The least?"

"Yup."

"What's the punch line?"

"It's a musical."

Shit.

Dawson picked up my mood pretty quickly the next morning in assembly. We'd had the first play practice, and it was going to really suck. I was going to have to sing seven songs in *Children of Eden*. He saw the same humor in my anointed new afternoon activity. It seemed everyone was going to get a good chuckle out of this except me.

"Have you ever acted before?"

"Only at home to avoid getting into trouble."

"What role are you?"

"I'm God."

Dawson smiled. He readily recognized the absurdity given our previous conversation.

"It's a musical, right?"

"Yeah."

"You're going to be a singing God?"

"Right again."

"You do see the irony in this, don't you?"

"I haven't missed it."

By then Abby had settled into her seat with the usual orchestra of bags, books, and chewing gum.

"So what did I miss so far?"

"Will's playing God in the spring musical."

"Do you know how to sing?"

"No."

"Have you ever acted?"

"No."

"I take it that you didn't volunteer for this part."

"Bussmann found a way to get even with me for belting him."

"Where can I get tickets?"

We had six weeks to prepare. In addition to the seven songs, I had ninety-seven lines to learn. Not to mention my usual homework, which was looking more and more appealing by the day. I wasn't sure if I would have stage fright because I really hadn't been on stage since elementary school. But I had a huge fear of the enormity of the work that had been set before me.

I didn't really believe I could get this done.

So my big problem now was learning how to sing and act. It's really hard to be the lead in a musical when you can't sing. I could be pretty good in front of the mirror in the bathroom. But standing in front of real people was likely to be a completely different story. My voice was high to begin with and got even higher when I sang. I don't think anyone ever expected God to sound like a kindergarten girl. And I don't remember seeing anything in the Bible about God's voice cracking.

Even remembering all of the lines to the songs was really hard. You couldn't fake it. Either you knew the lines or you didn't. And after a couple of weeks, I wasn't even close. We practiced each afternoon, just like sports. Only sports was lots easier. So while all the other kids were running around on the playing fields, I was humming the lines to the songs I was supposed to be learning. Humming because I didn't know the words.

"So how's God doing?"

"Not so great."

"How come?"

"God can't sing."

"How about if I help you?"

"You sing?"

"Better than you might expect."

"So how come you aren't in the play?"

"I don't do organized activities."

"So I've noticed. Why is that, anyway?"

"I march to my own tune."

"Again, so I've noticed."

"I'm worried about you. It doesn't look like you're up to the challenge."

I paused. Jelly was right. I was in way over my head.

"I don't think I can do this. There are four weeks left, and I only know one of the songs and probably about half my lines. And that's only during practice, when I have the chance to correct myself."

"What does Mr. McKenzie have to say?"

Mr. McKenzie was a music teacher who doubled as the director of the play. He lived for this stuff.

"He hasn't said as much, but I suspect he believes he is going down with the ship. He probably won't be talking to Buzzsaw for a long time."

"Have you talked to Bussmann about this? "

"I tried to after class last week. He said something about this being one of those steps that needed to be taken in order to grow up. I could certainly think of a lot of other options."

"Okay, so you and I will get together for extra practice every day. I'll coach you through this."

"I don't have any free time. I am barely getting my homework done as it is."

"We'll meet at six o'clock in the music room every morning."

"You'd get up at six for me?"

Jelly looked at me half grinning and half serious.

"Willy, there are a lot of things I would do for you. You just don't know that yet."

I got to school when it was still dark. My dad was thrilled to bring me since he thought it was a newfound intellectual curiosity. I knew it wasn't that. Spending time alone with Jelly would be the only reason I could ever think of for getting to school that early every morning. So I got up on time the first morning and every morning after that. It wasn't as difficult as I had anticipated. She was a good carrot. But she was going to have to be one hell of a coach to get me over this one.

"You know, there actually is hope for you."

"Right."

"I'm serious. When your voice doesn't crack, it's actually not bad. When did you say puberty is coming?"

"Not soon enough."

"Let's start at the beginning."

Jelly took the lead, and I willingly followed. I even surprised myself in how much I liked our sessions. Jelly was getting more out of me than any teacher ever had previously. I actually found that I didn't want to disappoint her. So we worked and worked. For the next twenty-eight days, including weekends, we met for almost two hours each day to rehearse. It was more concentrated time than I had spent on anything in my entire life. My preference still would have been to stay as far away as possible from the theater, but spending all that time alone with Jelly admittedly raised all sorts of other curiosities—even though this was strictly business.

"You have to remember to enunciate your words. There's a whole audience out there that needs to hear what you are saying. They don't have a script."

"Can't I just wave to them and move on?"

"Nice try. Okay, one more time from the top."

Best drill sergeant I ever had. And even at six o'clock in the morning she looked hot.

17.

When I had first arrived at Pendy, I got nauseous most mornings for the first month or so. It was a stressful introduction to the new place, and I felt the physical manifestations. Leading up to the show, I got incredible headaches. The night before the show even my teeth hurt. It was something like I had never experienced before. I'm sure it was the unfamiliar fear of being an actor up on stage in front of an audience. I would have rather been any place but there.

Jelly was in the front row. She wanted to see what all her early morning efforts with me had produced. Unlike the rest of the kids who came in packs for the Friday night social event, Jelly sat by herself. If she dressed more normally, she would have been mistaken for a teacher. My parents were a few rows behind her. I was glad that up to this point they had not yet met. I was feeling enough pressure already.

Unfortunately, I failed her as a pupil.

The play sucked. Or I should say that I sucked, and, as a result, the play sucked. I actually knew my lines reasonably well thanks to Jelly. I simply melted under pressure. Getting up on stage at practice wasn't fun, but it was something that I could get through. Put a packed audience in front of me, however, and there was no hope. I got confused on the first song, stumbled a few times on the second song, and it was downhill from there. By the end I was back to just kind of humming. Once again, I wasn't cool under pressure.

When Mr. McKenzie screamed at me during intermission, I, of course, teared up, and they had to reapply my makeup. By the final curtain, everyone was ticked at me. While theater was my punishment, it was their basketball. And they had just gotten the beating of their lives.

So I resolved that I would just go back deeper into my already deep shell.

*IT WAS UNFAIR TO put Will up on stage like that. I felt his pain with
every line he mumbled or hummed. It was pretty embarrassing, and
I doubt the other kids in school were going to let him forget what was
likely the most miserable acting performance the school had ever seen. I
knew I wouldn't forget it any time soon. At the end of the show, I was
actually hoping to sneak out of the auditorium without having to speak
with any of the other parents. They weren't going to be congratulating
me, that was for sure. In fact, they were probably pissed at me, too, for
not raising a more capable kid.*

*When I dropped him off at school every morning at six for a month, he
said that he was practicing for the play. I had no reason not to believe
him. Hell, Will had never woken up that early for anything in his life.
What I couldn't figure out was how after that much practice he was still
so bad. I didn't think that I was overestimating his capabilities. But
maybe I was. He really was awful up there.*

*It seemed easier for other parents. I'd always watch them with their kids.
It seemed to me that they just pulled up their cars at the curb in front of
the Main School each morning and dropped off organized, motivated
students. Their hair was combed, their backpacks were neat, and they
didn't grunt at each other. My kid looked like he was still in bed. Will's
mother, Amy, and I had always done well in school. We went to good*

colleges, got good grades and did well in our careers. Amy gave up her job to raise our kids, but she was smart and had an incredible work ethic. It didn't seem Will had gotten any of our genes when it came to school. Though we used his middle name, he was named after me. But the similarities increasingly seemed to end with our name.

Every night I lived with this anxiety that Will had forgotten to do one of his subjects for homework or wasn't fully prepared for a test the next day. Initially I would try to ask a few questions early in the evening to try to gauge his readiness. The questions turned to hints as the evening evolved until finally I would end up far too many nights just lecturing him. It was as if I were doing the worrying rather than Will. I didn't know if I was going to be able to take four years of this. It was brutal. And while Amy had begun to question whether Pendy was the right school for him, I wasn't yet ready to quit.

CLASS III

"Hey, stranger."

"Hey."

"How was your summer?"

"Good."

"Miss me?"

"Of course."

"You've grown."

"It's called puberty."

"Yeah? Well it's working. You're cuter than ever. You've got an even hotter ass now."

I may have had a hot ass now, but Jelly looked phenomenal. She had a totally new look. Her hair was orange this time. Not like the Irish kids with freckles orange, but Halloween pumpkin orange. She had grown it longer, down to her shoulders, now in an even length all the way around. She looked more grown up than when she had the lopsided mop of the year before.

She, too, had matured noticeably matured. Her boobs were bigger, and her body had a new contour to it. She was no longer a boy with earrings.

"Guess what?" she continued.

"What?"

I couldn't help smiling. She was actually happy to see me. No female under forty had ever been happy to see me before.

"I've got some big news. I'm living in the Fort."

"Really?"

"Really."

"How come?"

"Trouble in paradise. The lesbians are fighting—probably splitting up. Not such a fun place to be. So they let me come here."

"That kind of surprises me."

"How come?"

"I figured that lesbians generally got along better than regular couples."

"As opposed to irregular couples."

"You know what I mean."

"So what makes you think that they would get along better?"

"Just think about how much more stuff they have to put up with. I mean, they probably disappointed their parents, who must have thought it was weird their not being straight. When they were growing up, other kids probably made fun of them behind their backs. Heck, my parents still stare at gay couples and make spiteful remarks about their being from 'the dark side.' And my grandparents are way worse. I figured that if gay couples can get through all that crap, they should be able to survive any normal relationship problems that might come up."

"You actually may have a point."

"I didn't offend you, did I?

"You never do."

"You don't think they are going to make it?"

"It's a pretty good row." She knew I had never heard that term before. "When you get that one right on your SATs you can thank me."

"Who would you end up living with?"

"I don't know. I never thought of that."

"Which one is actually your mom?"

"What do you mean?"

"You know, which one actually gave birth to you?"

"Hardy."

"Really?"

"Yeah."

"I would have guessed Laurel."

"Why?"

"Probably because you told me that Hardy has a mustache."

We stood outside the Main School, early for the year's first assembly. From a weather standpoint, it was still summer. Even that early in the morning the humidity had my dress shirt already beginning to stick to my back. It was hard to believe that in four weeks leaves would be falling off trees. Jelly wore a lime green tank top, baggy skirt, and a new pair of canvas high top sneakers. She hugged her backpack in front of her belly and rocked her body side to side as we spoke. There was endless lawn around the entrance to the Main School, yet she stood no more than three feet in front of me.

Though Jelly would always look different from the other girls, I wasn't taken aback this year. Her orange hair was shocking but not unattractive. She had lost some of the earrings, and, from the looks of it, she had lost her bra too. The unencumbered spirit in her. I was certainly more comfortable arriving at school this year, but my blue jacket and khaki slacks uniform was the same as in the past. She was going to keep it interesting.

"So what did you do this summer?" I asked.

"Went to camp."

"For how long?"

"The whole summer."

"Really?"

"Uh huh."

"Was it fun?"

"Yeah, it was pretty good."

"Where was it?"

"Paris."

"France?"

"Last time I looked."

"I've only been out of New England once."

"La meilleur facon d'eviter les maladies du foie, c'est de manger convenablement."

"Huh?"

"I said, 'The best way to avoid a stomach ache is to eat sensibly.'"

"I get queasy just walking into assembly."

I couldn't help but notice her bosoms. Though bigger than last year, they were still small relative to a lot of the girls in the school. But boobs were boobs. I had never realized how much impact a bra had on fashioning their shape. With a bra, they were rounded and symmetrical. Without the harness, they hung lower and without a traditional geometry, readily willing to lean to the left or right depending upon which way she rocked.

"So what do you think?"

She knew I was looking.

"Pretty nice, I guess."

"If I had asked you that last year, you would have blushed."

"If we keep this conversation up, I'll probably start blushing pretty soon, too."

"You are soooo cute."

"Okay. I'm gonna blush now."

"Have you ever thought about what it would be like to fool around with me?"

"Uh huh."

"That didn't take long for you to think about."

"Lately I've thought about fooling around with pretty much any girl who talks to me."

She laughed.

"But I'm the only girl you really ever talk to."

"So I guess that puts you in a class by yourself. But remember, I only get to think about it."

"Maybe your luck will change this year."

"I doubt it."

"That's not a very positive attitude."

"Can we change the subject?"

"Are you going to blush again?"

"Or get sick to my stomach."

"I can be so mean, can't I?"

"You have your moments. But for some reason, I'm still glad to see you."

20.

"Will!"

"Hey, Shaky."

"Man, what happened to you?"

I just smiled.

"You could be bigger than me now."

"Shaky, there isn't anybody on campus bigger than you. Have a good summer?"

He was certainly no smaller than last year and now sported a pencil-thin beard that stretched from one ear, under the point of his chin and back up to the other ear. It was as if someone had taken a marker pen and drawn a chin strap on his face. It probably took him about three days to grow.

"It was alright."

"What'd you do?"

"Nothing. Hung mostly."

"Me too."

"Really pissed ma grandma off."

"I hear you. My parents canceled the cable television."

"We don't get cable. My grandma thinks it's too violent. She oughta look out the window sometime. She volunteered me ta paint the church."

"That kinda blows."

"Yeah, hopefully it'll count for some of my community service hours. 'Cause they didn't pay me shit."

All students were required to do eighty hours of community service at some point during their four years at Pendy. It was supposed to keep us humble.

"Go to any Red Sox games?"

"Three. You?"

"Two, but both were against the Yankees."

"Yeah. I couldn't sneak inta those. Too many security guys."

"You sneak into Fenway?"

"Sure 'nuff. I'll take you someday. It's cheaper. How's Purple Hair?"

"It's orange now."

"She still got a thing for you?"

"We're just friends."

"Yeah, right."

"Remember, she's a lesbian."

"So she says."

"I think it's genetic in her case. Both parents are."

"Too bad."

"I guess. Nice beard, by the way."

"Think the girls are gonna think it's hot?"

"I doubt it."

"Yeah, me too. But I didn't have no luck last year, so I thought I'd try a new look."

It felt good to see Shaky. Next to Jelly, he was my best friend at school. I never stayed in touch with any of the kids over the summer. I didn't have my license yet, so getting together was too much work. Besides, I wouldn't even know how to get to Shaky's apartment. Dorchester might as well have been on another continent from where I lived.

Sometimes, when I actually thought about it, I would feel sorry for Shaky. For as confident as he outwardly appeared to be—just like Jelly, he was way more confident than I could ever imagine being—it had to be hard to be at a school with so many rich kids. My family was pretty well off, and I felt poor next to most of the people here. Shaky had little. I'm sure being at Pendy was a good opportunity for him, better than any of the public high schools in Boston. But Shaky was over his head here, and he knew it. He did worse in his classes than I did. He wasn't very smart, and he didn't study. Not a great combination. Clearly he was on a free ride here, yet he didn't seem to care. If I had been in his shoes I probably would have felt cheated. His classmates, supposedly his friends, would drive home to their McMansions in nice cars each night after sports while he would take the bus back to his grandmother's apartment to sleep on her couch.

"What are you gonna do for a sport this fall?"

"Probably cross-country again. You?"

"No way. I'm not made for that sport. I'll probably pretend I'm hurt all season or something. Thought you wanted to play football."

"I do. But my mother doesn't want me to play. She thinks I'm too skinny and will get hurt. And I don't know how to play soccer."

"That makes two 'a us. Hey, it'll give you more time to get your work done, right?" A quick smile from the big boy.

"That's what I was afraid of."

"Want to go up to the turret?"

21.

I still didn't really like school. I mean, I had some decent acquaintances, and I liked hanging with Shaky and Jelly when they weren't being too crazy. And I liked playing basketball. But school was so constant. Get up. Carpool to school. Assembly. Sit in class, eat lunch, sit in more class, sports, and homework. I really hated homework. It never went away. I still wasted incredible amounts of time while I was supposed to be doing homework. I knew it, but there was nothing I could do about it. I knew that I should have been taking it more seriously. I mean, I didn't want to do poorly, but I had no motivation. I wasn't any better second year than I'd been the first.

While Pendy wasn't my favorite place in the world, I did feel like I at least belonged by my sophomore year. A big part of it was that I wasn't such a shrimp anymore. I had started to grow at an epic rate and would eat every chance I got just to fuel my growth for the day. I'd eat two lunches at school whenever I had an extra free period. At night I'd have a snack every hour on the hour between dinner and bedtime.

"You find something to eat?"

"Peanut butter and cheese."

"That's sounds appealing."

"It's actually not bad. It's all we have in the house."

"Will, grocery shopping is the worst. I never know what to get you. Want to come with me sometime?"

"No thanks, Mom. Just use this rule of thumb—if you think it's unhealthy, then get lots of it."

"Great."

We were all in the kitchen. My mother was doing the dishes. My father was at the table eating cereal and reading the sports page. Unlike me, he worked pretty hard. He had just gotten home from a late meeting at work. It was sort of a still photo of the now traditional American family.

"So, Mom, can I have a cell phone?"

No longer being such a physical anomaly, I was also planning on becoming slightly more curious socially. Not that I would ever be fodder for a reality television show, but I was entertaining the thought of abandoning my status as a monk.

"Ask your father."

"Dad, can I have a cell phone?"

"No."

Okay, let's try instant replay.

"Mommmm? Can I please have a cell phone?"

"I said ask your father."

"He said no."

"Michael, is a cell phone actually so bad?"

"I don't want him killed."

"Dad, cell phones haven't murdered anyone in years. Honest. I checked all the newspapers."

"Nice try, wise ass. You'll be wanting your learner's permit soon. Cars and cell phones are a bad combination."

"You talk on your phone in the car."

"He's right, Michael. And I hate when you do that."

"I'm a more experienced driver."

"How about if I promise not to take it in the car?"

"And who are you planning to have pay for it?"

"How much does it cost?"

"Probably seventy-five dollars for a phone and twenty bucks a month for service."

"Okay, then you can pay for it."

"I'm already paying for that expensive school of yours."

"Hey, you were the one who wanted me to go there. I'll go to the public high school, and you can buy me a cell phone. It'll save you a bunch of money."

"No deal."

"How about if I make honors?

"Deal."

Now, I knew I had absolutely no chance of making honors, but at least the door was not completely shut.

22.

PUBERTY IS AN AMAZING thing. I watched as Will matured daily before my eyes. He was not a man yet, but he wasn't a little kid anymore. In less than a year he'd grown eight inches to an even six feet tall. We'd had to buy him all new clothes for the school year as nothing from last year even came close to fitting. He had the beginnings of a little black, peach fuzz mustache, but no signs of hair under his arms or on his legs as best as I could tell.

While his room was a total disaster—I was playing under the assumption that this was the case with most high school kids—he did seem to care a little more about his personal appearance, which was a step in the right direction. I couldn't tell if it was that friend of his or if he was just growing up. But he showered most days and seemed to change his underwear and socks reasonably regularly. He spent noticeably more time in front of the mirror combing his hair to make sure that it was agreeably messy and checking out his biceps.

On our way home from church one Sunday at the end of the summer, he told me that he didn't believe in God. This was a revelation, one I was not prepared to deal with. I could understand any misgivings he might have had about the Catholic Church. After all, they were screwing it up pretty well. But he leaped right over that point, going directly to the atheist angle. I gave him the best speech I could muster on the short *notice—talking about the need for values and how blessed our family had been in life—but he clearly didn't buy any of it. Whenever Will thought my speeches were ill intended, he'd just tune out and grunt. He'd done some hall of fame grunting during this one.*

Unfortunately, he didn't seem to be gaining any newfound interest in his schoolwork. Academics were a labor to him, and, unfortunately, not a labor of love. He was the least organized, least dedicated student I had ever seen. He was far different than I was in my youth. The kid had brains, but he sure didn't like to drag them out of the closet very often.

We had always thought that we would be great parents. We expected that if we were good role models, kept a little discipline in the house, and showed the kids a lot of love, they would follow our leads. It was more exasperating than I'd ever imagined.

23.

AFTER OUR CONVERSATION THE previous year while painting backdrops for the school play, I'd begun to build a bit of a relationship with Dawson. Most of our conversations occurred during assembly, the one place we saw each other and were forced to sit together each day. He didn't squeak as much anymore and sometimes looked at me instead of his feet.

I remained amazed how fresh and awake he was each morning. He was the one kid who wore his clothes the right way. His shirt was always pressed and tucked inside his pants. His tie had a perfect Windsor knot, and he wore dress shoes every day rather than sneakers, like most of us. I usually looked like I'd just rolled out of bed, which was most often the case.

"So how come you are always walking around school taking pictures?"

"I didn't think anyone noticed."

"I notice a lot more than most people here."

"Really?"

"It's one of my unique skills."

His comment unnerved me just a little. I had been assuming I was still mostly invisible.

"You hide behind walls and buildings, and you climb trees at night," he continued. "It's not normal high school behavior."

"I never claimed to be a normal high school kid."

Dawson paused at my comment and didn't say anything more for a while.

"So what are you doing?"

"Taking pictures."

"For class?"

"Mostly, I guess. I just like photography a lot. I'm trying to get better at it."

"Your approach is a little weird, don't you think?"

"I can see how you might think that. But we all have our own ways of doing things."

He knew I was talking more about him. But I figured it would give me a way to change the subject. I liked photography a lot, but it was still kind of a personal thing, so I really didn't know how to talk about it. Plus I didn't much like talking about me.

"So did you go to church this morning?" I asked.

"Of course."

"Do other kids go too?"

"A few."

"What do you actually do there every morning?"

"Read the scriptures. Pray. Talk to God."

"You talk to God?"

"In my own way."

"Does he answer?"

"Sometimes yes and sometimes no."

"You still like that stuff, don't you?"

"Yeah, very much."

"I wish I could have such a strong conviction about something. I just really don't understand the relevance of religion."

"You might be surprised if you spent some time with Him."

"I'm not sure I agree with you."

"Want to come with me some morning?"

"What time would I have to be there?"

"Six o'clock."

"If I said yes now, I would just be acting nice. I can't see getting up that early to go to church."

"I understand. If you change your mind, just let me know. It's my best part of the day."

His best part of the day. Either Dawson's days were pretty lame or I was really missing out on something.

24.

I FINALLY GOT MY cell phone. I didn't make honors the first quarter, but I'd spent the previous month working more hours than I ever had. Or at least I seemed to be working more hours. Mostly I was playing solitaire and checkers on my computer and scouring the Internet. But my parents thought that I had found a new work ethic. Several nights I went to bed after midnight, the computer always purring, me always sitting in front of the screen feigning concentration. They were proud of my work ethic for the first time in my high school career. So they bought me a cell phone as a reward.

Cell phones are amazing things. They open up a whole new world—a world of immediacy. Whatever was happening, I could know about it. A national catastrophe, a good joke, a clandestine party. Cell phone circuits challenged the speed of light. Not that I got invited to any of the clandestine parties, but the potential, at least, was now there.

The cell phone became the beginning of a new and exciting chapter for me. If my parents had only known.

"Hi, cutey."

"Jelly, it's one-thirty. What are you doing calling me?" I was whispering at the top of my lungs.

"I thought you'd be asleep."

"I was lying in bed, trying to sleep."

"With your cell phone in your hand?"

"Actually it was under my pillow."

"You sleep with your cell phone under your pillow?"

"In case anybody calls."

"Isn't this more fun than trying to sleep?"

"Truthfully?"

"Uh huh."

"Yeah it is. I wasn't really tired yet anyway. Most nights I just lie in bed till about two before I fall asleep."

"So what are you wearing?"

"To bed?"

"I didn't think you were at a prom or anything."

"My boxers and a t-shirt."

"I bet you look sexy."

"Hardly."

Jelly was amazing. She theoretically didn't even like guys, yet she could flirt like nobody I had ever met. And I couldn't believe I was lying in bed at one-thirty and talking with her. My parents would have killed me if they'd known. Fortunately my room was at the other end of the house from theirs, but I was still careful to whisper.

"So guess what I'm wearing?"

"Now?"

"Man, you're a little slow."

"Besides your orange hair?"

"Nice try."

"A bra?"

"Hardly." She laughed at my line, getting the full humor.

"So what then?"

"Nothing."

"You're naked?"

"Yup."

"You sleep naked?"

"No. But I thought it would be fun to call you naked. Thought I could get a rise out of you." She was certainly succeeding in that, but I wasn't going to tell her. "Why don't you try it next time I call?"

"Is this gonna be a regular thing?"

"I don't know. You'll just have to wait and see, won't you." There was a pause. "Uuuup. Gotta go. Footsteps in the hallway. Bye, lovey."

And that was it.

I stayed awake a long time that night. The vision of Jelly naked was the only thing filling my mind. I had never seen a fully naked woman for real before. Not even my mother.

25.

I LOOKED FOR JELLY the next day in school but didn't see her anywhere. Probably in the back of my mind I foolishly expected to see her walking around campus with no clothes. Like my first year, we weren't in any of the same classes, but we still tried to run into each other every day—at assembly, at lunch, between classes, or before sports.

But she wasn't in assembly or lunch that day. Nor the next one for that matter. I knew I should have called her, but she was always the instigator in our relationship. I was comfortable with that arrangement. But after waiting three days I got up the guts.

"Hi, it's me."

Clearly she'd been crying.

"What's the matter?" I asked.

"Laurel and Hardy."

"Huh?"

"They split."

"Oh … I'm sorry."

"What a couple of shits."

"Yeah, I guess that kind of sucks."

"They want to share me."

"What do you mean?"

"They want to cut me down the fucking middle and each take half! One day with one and the next day with the other. They are fucking arguing about it in front of me! Lesbians can be mean fucking narcissists."

"As usual, I don't even know what that means."

"Don't worry. You don't want to."

"Can I help in any way?"

"Can you make two wack jobs stop screaming at each other!"

"I didn't know you'd be so upset."

"Wouldn't you if your parents were splitting up and tearing each other's hearts out in the process!"

I had never thought about my parents getting divorced. When I came into the world, they were a pair. And, in my mind, I figured that they would always be that. I had always assumed they had a good relationship, but as I thought more about it, I realized I really didn't know. In my mind, being a mother or a father was sort of like a job. It was their profession, and except for my father's almost psychotic hovering over my schoolwork, they seemed to do a reasonably good job at it. I didn't know how I would have felt if they split. I mean, I'm sure that I would have been sad, but I didn't know if I would have been overly emotional or not.

"I really am sorry."

"They're such assholes!"

After another couple of minutes of my uninspiring commentary I hung up. I certainly wasn't helping as I had no idea what to say. Interestingly, I realized that I really did want to help her, which was unusual for me. I wasn't really the helpful type.

I thought that night a lot about Jelly's life being torn in two by her parents. I also thought about Dawson and how his most meaningful relationship was at a nonearthly level. Nothing on this earth, it seemed, was going to splinter that relationship. Not a father lording over him, not feuding parents, not a romance that had no chance of ever coming to fruition. At least, that's the way it seemed to me. Maybe I was wrong. Maybe he was the strongest of us all.

Eventually Jelly came back to school, but she wasn't her usual self for a while. Nonetheless, she had started me down a path, in her absence, of which I was none too proud but found very hard to stop despite my feelings of guilt. It turned out that the Internet was one big porn channel. Google anything you want—nip slips, breasts, fully naked women. You name it, and it was there. It began to seriously cut into my studying time.

COMMUNITY SERVICE WAS THE big, new requirement in prep schools. It was required to graduate. All the schools touted their service programs in their glossy brochures. It was their way of training tomorrow's leaders to take responsibility for their citizenship.

Pendy's students had to do eighty hours of community service during their four years. By my calculations, that came to three minutes and twenty-nine seconds per day. I understood the intent. But my sense was that the execution did not live up to the marketing hype. For the rich kids, community service was just another vacation. Four thousand dollars for a trip via a for-profit company to build houses on an Indian reservation in New Mexico or work with school age kids in St. Lucia in between the golf and snorkeling of a family vacation. And I was pretty certain that doing good for three minutes a day wasn't going to reshape who we were.

Then there was Shaky. My classmates should have been doing community service for him.

I knew there was no chance my parents were ever going to pay for a trip. In fact, in my own mind I could never even justify it. So I saw an ad in our town newspaper recruiting for volunteers to teach illiterate people. It sounded interesting. Someone who'd be less of a student than me. I could handle that.

"Hi."

"I'm Will."

"I'm Carl."

Carl was thirty-eight. He couldn't read.

"I heard you want to learn some stuff."

"I need to get my GED."

"Is that the high school equivalency test?"

"Uh huh."

"You never graduated from high school?"

"No."

"Did you ever go to high school?"

"Six years."

"How come you didn't graduate?"

"I didn't go to class very often."

"So what's made you want to get your diploma now?"

"I need to get a better job. I've been bagging groceries for nineteen years."

"I guess we have some work to do."

"Think you can help me learn to read?"

"I can try."

"How about math?"

"Not very good at it?"

"You'll see."

"Okay, we'll give it a try."

"I may need some help in history too."

"History?"

"It's on the GED."

"You've taken the test before?"

"Twice."

"No luck."

"Not even close."

"Have you ever been tutored before?"

"This is my first time."

I had the sinking feeling this was going to take way more than eighty hours.

"So I guess we can meet on Sunday afternoons. One o'clock work?"

"Can we make it a little later? My brother doesn't get up too early on Sundays, and I need him to give me a ride."

"You don't drive?"

"Can't read. Can't pass the written part of the driving test."

"Do you know how to drive?"

"I'm a great driver. But I got busted a couple of times for driving without a license. Can't risk that anymore."

"Mind if I ask how much money you earn bagging groceries?"

"Eight seventy-five an hour."

After nineteen years.

"What do you want to do after you learn to read?"

"Be a hairdresser."

"Really?"

"Yeah. I think I'd be pretty good at it."

"Do you have to be able to read to be a hairdresser?"

"Have to have your GED to go to beauty school."

He actually did have pretty nice hair. It was thick and long with graying curls around the ears. His salt and pepper mustache was meticulously trimmed. It was hard to believe he was illiterate.

"Think you can help me?" he asked again.

"I guess I can try."

"Thanks."

"Are you going to show up for all of our tutoring sessions?"

"Absolutely."

27.

"Hı."

"What the hell time is it?"

I'd been sleeping with my cell phone under my pillow ever since her first wake-up call.

"Two."

"Shit."

"I'm back."

"To what?"

"To being me."

"I'm glad to hear it."

"Sorry about being such a bitch."

"Hey, you've had tough stuff to deal with."

"It is what it is. So you want to do something?"

"Sure. When?"

"How about now?"

"Now?"

"Uh huh."

"It's two o'clock!"

"It's a nice night."

"It's almost morning."

"Are you chicken?"

"Yes."

"What's the risk? I'll come by in my car and pick you up."

"My parents will kill me."

"I'll tell you what. I'm going to be out for a drive. I'll swing by your house. If you're out, we'll go somewhere. If not, no big deal."

"You're kidding me."

"Hey, no pressure."

"I always feel pressure with you. You're going to give me a coronary!"

I lay in bed after hanging up, thinking of a million reasons why I shouldn't do this. But I knew from the start I would. The old Jelly was back. I would be happy to see her.

Getting out of the house was not hard. I threw on some sweats, grabbed some of my mother's breath gum from her purse, and snuck down the back stairs and out the door that led to a brick patio in our backyard. Once outside, I popped on my sneakers, which I had been carrying in my hand, and crept around to the front of the house to wait by a lamppost on the street. It was early November, and the night was colder out than I had planned for. I pulled my sweatshirt hood over my head and folded my arms across my chest to try to stop the shivering. I had only to wait about fifteen minutes before Jelly's little red Civic came trucking down the street to pick me up. I quickly hopped in.

"Glad you could make it."

"Hope the heat's on."

"Cold out there?"

"Like a witch's you know what."

"I wasn't sure you'd be out."

"I shouldn't be."

"Do I have that kind of magic over you?"

"Apparently."

"You still look pretty cute for the middle of the night."

"I doubt that. And I'm not blushing this time."

"Nervous?"

"Absolutely."

"And kind of excited?"

"Kind of."

"Good."

"Where're we going?"

"I have no idea."

"You called me at two in the morning, and you have no idea where we're going?"

"You were wondering if I was naked when I called, weren't you?"

"How did we switch to that subject?"

"Tell the truth."

"I plead the fifth."

"Thought so."

Jelly was back. Almost. She certainly walked to a drummer different from most kids', but a weeknight escape was still a little out of character, even for her.

"You like the beach?"

"In the summer."

"Want to go?"

"Now?"

"Why not?"

"Do I have a choice?"

"Nope. You are under my spell now."

We drove for a while without talking. Fortunately she seemed to know where we were going, since I had absolutely no clue. We drove on the Mass Pike for a bit, I knew that much. After that, if she would have dropped me on the side of the road, there was no way I could have found my way home. Ultimately, she pulled her car into a deserted parking lot next to a beach. As she did, she reached under her seat and pulled out a grocery bag. From inside of it, she pulled out a beer, offering it to me.

"Want one?"

"Where are we?"

"Southie. South Boston. That's the L Street Bathhouse."

"I don't know what that is."

"Supposedly that is where the Boston mob guys hang out. You've heard of Whitey Bulger, haven't you?"

"I think so."

"Kind of neat, isn't it?"

"That you brought me to drink beer in the middle of the night with mobsters?"

"You don't have to drink."

"How did you find this place?"

"I have an aunt who lives a couple of blocks from here."

"Are you planning on us visiting her tonight too?"

"Not tonight. So you want to try one?"

She had already popped a can open and was taking a long swallow from it. She'd done this before.

"Why not? I've broken every other rule tonight."

The first beer didn't go down without some labor on my part. I can't say that I liked the taste; I would have preferred Dr Pepper. But it was kind of a novel sensation.

"Why did we come out here tonight?" I asked.

"I don't know. I needed a break. Every once in a while I have to push the edge to see if I still have it."

"Are you planning to include me in all these little ventures?"

"You don't want me to?"

"I'm not sure, to tell you the truth."

"You shouldn't be scared."

"That's easy for you to say. You're way more experienced in this stuff than I am."

"I'll protect you."

"I hope so. I do better when it's light out."

There was a certain peacefulness to this parking lot in the shadows of Whitey Bulger's hangout. I should have been scared, but I really wasn't. Maybe it was the beer. Maybe it was having the original Jelly back. It was like time stopped for a few moments, and I could just enjoy having no accountability.

"How's the catfight going?"

"They seem to be calming down. At least it's livable again."

"It made me wonder how I'd feel if my parents split up."

"I don't think that you have to worry about that. *Happy Days* reruns, remember?"

"How could I forget? Still, it got me thinking. I couldn't figure if I'd be upset or not. I mean, it would certainly be a change, but I don't know if it would really affect me that much."

"They're your parents. You've been a unit your whole life. It sort of shakes you to the core. You see each of them in a different light than you ever have before. And trust me, it's not that pretty."

"I'm sorry you're having to go through all this."

"I know you are."

"So do you mind if I change the subject?"

"Out here we can talk about anything you want."

"What's your view on God?"

"Wow! Where the hell did that one come from?"

"I'm actually serious. I've been talking a little more to Dawson lately. He goes to church every morning before school and claims he talks to God. I'm not sure I know what to make of it, but he certainly thinks that something magical happens in his life because of it."

"This may be a little too heavy for the middle of the night."

"I know. It's probably too heavy for the middle of the day too. But I have been known to show a bit of gravitas from time to time."

"SAT word?"

"Of course."

"Well, to answer your question, I have never been to church in my life. Any kind of church. And I've never even talked about religion with Laurel or Hardy. But I do believe that there is some kind of spiritual being out there watching over us."

"Really?"

"Sure. How else do you explain all of this stuff around us?"

"The good stuff or the bad stuff?"

"Man, you can be deeper than I thought."

"That's not such a terrible thing, is it?"

"No, Willy. Not at all."

After carefully nursing the first beer of my life, the second beer proved to be a different story. It went down fine. Unfortunately, when we started to drive home, it started to find its way back up.

"Pull over. I think I'm going to be sick."

I got sick on the side of the road in Southie, in Milton, in Westwood, and in Needham. It was more than a little embarrassing. I had Jelly, the only girl I had ever had a crush on, to myself, and I was making a total fool of myself. By the time I got back to Wellesley, there was nothing left to get sick with.

"You gonna be okay?"

"Yeah, sorry about all this."

"My fault. I shouldn't have made you come with me."

"It's okay. It was fun—except for the puking part."

"I guess we'll have to do it again then."

I crept back into the house. The clock above the stove was shining 5:40 in blue neon. I had to be up in an hour to shower and change. I removed my shoes and meandered quietly up the back stairs to my room. Still drunk and still nauseous. Once inside the room, I pulled off my sweatshirt and slid into bed.

I was almost asleep when I became aware that someone else was in my room. A silhouette in the chair across the floor where I usually threw my clothes from the day. I leaped up and flicked on the lamp on my nightstand. There sat my father in his suit and tie. Arms folded across his chest. I'd forgotten he was going on a trip to Cleveland that day. He was more angry than I had ever seen him.

28.

THE SCHOOL HAD A little glossy newspaper that came out every couple of weeks. I would take it up to the turret and read it on Wednesdays—after class but before sports. One week they wrote about a Pendy grad who was fighting in Iraq. Here was a guy who had been in my shoes just a few years before, taking the same courses with the same teachers that I had. Eating the same meals. His name was Juanier Lopez. He was Hispanic.

I tried to imagine who Juanier was. He didn't have to worry about picking up his room or doing homework. He didn't have to worry about being caught in a world between spoiled, rich kids like Hartford who could and would have whatever they wanted in life no matter what they did in school, and dirt poor kids like Shaky, who would keep getting free rides in high school, in college, and in his career because he was a disadvantaged minority. Juanier didn't have to figure out if he had a crush on a lesbian or not.

All Juanier Lopez had to worry about was keeping his head down and not getting shot. It didn't matter if he did his job well or not. One guy alone was not going to topple Sadaam Hussein, al-Qaida, or the Taliban insurgents. Even though I may have been the only one in the world who thought this, I thought his life was easier than mine. I mean, I readily admit I wasn't killing myself with effort, but the stress of being indifferent was beginning to get to me.

My dad grounded me for the rest of the year. There was no debate. I would go to school, do my sports, and unless I had to stay late for something academic related, come home. He would sit in a chair in my room and either read or do his own work each night while I did mine. Except for our traditional dissection of each basketball game I played, there wouldn't be much new or fun to our conversation. Sometimes I could get him to help me study for a test or write a paper for me. But it was suburban prison. I wasn't going to be sneaking out at night for a beer anymore, and my grades were going to go up. He was going to make sure of that.

Somewhere along the way, my father had come to the realization that grades in all courses—whether core courses or electives, advanced placement, honors, or classes for the dumb kids—counted the same in the grade point average. So he decided that I should keep taking photography each semester. He had never seen any of my photos or talked to my teacher, but clearly it was my best grade. So I kept taking it.

I didn't mind at all. Photography remained a great release, which I needed since my father had taken all of my usual distractions away. It wasn't really like schoolwork. All I had to do was push a button. I morphed into digital photography, the newer, better technology for taking pictures. While I was still amazed at how the old technology worked—how you could push a simple button and freeze time for all eternity to see—digital was more than incredible. The school actually provided the camera since the art teachers were beginning to experiment with the technology. I was good enough and readily willing to be their guinea pig.

I had decided that I was going to create my own yearbook of every kid in the school—taking pictures not posed and how they wanted to be seen, but rather as I saw them. I knew it could be incriminating as hell for some of the kids, and chances were that I would probably never show the pictures to anyone. But so many of the kids were so rich, so self-centered, and so focused on dressing themselves up to look good on their college applications, I thought it would be more remarkable to view them in a more realistic light. It would be easy and fun. All except Jelly. She was the only real one. She was the same in person as on camera. Her picture would probably just be a blank white space. I decided to leave the teachers out for the time being in case someone ever got hold of my yearbook. Might be too hard to explain.

"Are you taking pictures for the school newspaper?"

"Nope."

"Yearbook?"

"Not really."

"So what's with the Jimmy Olsen impersonation?"

"Superman's buddy?"

"That makes me Lois Lane."

"I've got to be honest with you. I don't see the similarity."

"Wiseass."

We both laughed. I actually thought it was pretty funny. Jelly loved to be photographed, and it still really pissed her off that I never took pictures of her. She was the offbeat one. The one who was not like every other girl in school—from her lesbian parents and her supposed girlfriends to her non-Gap clothing and green high tops. And she would have loved to have had it all chronicled.

She knew that relative to the rest of the kids at the school, I was a good photographer. They were going to create a new advanced placement digital photography course next year just for me. It would be the only way I would ever take an AP course. A lot of my pictures would hang in the school's hallways. But there were never any of Jelly. When I had my camera, it was the only time I ever had the advantage over her, the only time I was ever out from under her spell. Not that I didn't like being under her spell. I did. This was just different, and it felt kind of good to be in control in our strange relationship every once in a while.

"Really, what's with the new volume of pictures?" She tried again.

"Jealous?"

"Not as long as you finally take some pictures of me."

"We shall see."

"Seriously, though. You've been snapping like crazy."

"I didn't know anyone noticed."

"It would be hard not to."

"It's my new project. I'm creating my own yearbook."

"Huh?"

"People as I see them. Pendy according to Will."

"Uh oh. This could be interesting."

"I think so."

"Are you going to show me the pictures?"

"Of course. But just you."

"Will I like them?"

"You'll probably laugh."

"Will my picture be included?"

"Remains to be seen. By the way, are you planning to keep asking that same question?"

"You should know by now I rarely give up. It's another one of my better qualities. So are you going to turn it in for a grade?"

"Not a chance."

"So you spend more time on non-schoolwork than you do on schoolwork?"

"Kind of strange, isn't it?"

"I'll say."

"How are you going to get into college?"

"You sound like my parents."

"I'm serious."

"I didn't think you cared."

"Only about you, cutey."

"And my ass."

"And your ass."

The lens on the camera was bigger than the camera itself. It could see a great distance. With the days getting shorter during the winter of my sophomore year, I was able to wander about more freely, stealthily taking photos from the darkness, where I was invisible to the subject. I would tell my parents that I was staying after practice for extra help. In spite of my grounding, they would be thrilled. All the while I'd go on my walkabouts, looking for the side of students the rest of the world never saw.

Jessie Grabow, the one who Shaky had witnessed in her sleep, would sneak off into the great cross-country woods after practice with a few of her friends periodically and smoke dope until they could no longer control their giggling. Had pictures of the whole group with doobers in their hands. Jenny was a third generation Princeton legacy.

Dawson was a Peeping Tom who would go out in the dark after sports and look in the windows of the faculty houses. I think he mostly liked to look into kids' rooms.

Derek Moriarity, captain of the football team, was rumored to be applying early decision to Harvard in December. He lived on the second floor of the Fort. I got a picture of him through his window masturbating to some girly magazine. He didn't think anyone could see through his window. He obviously also didn't think anyone would climb trees at night and sit there waiting for such opportunistic pictures.

While I sat in the tree I always looked through the camera lens at Jelly. The window to her room was directly above the Harvard-bound masturbator. I would watch and watch, knowing that if the right picture came up that I would probably break my promise to myself and take her picture. But during all my hours in the tree, the right picture never came up. She just sat at her desk and studied— underlining sentences in the textbooks as she read, typing away at papers on her computer, pecking at her calculator as she knocked out problem sets for math. She had incredible powers of concentration and a discipline I'd never before witnessed. I would wait and wait for her to do the something wild as expected, as if she really knew that I was secretly watching her and wanted her to perform for me as she always did. But it never happened.

The class president was a guy named Greg Masterson. He was without a doubt the best looking guy I had ever seen. I don't think I was worried about my sexuality, but his presence was hard to deny. In his blue blazer and khakis, he could have passed for being thirty years old. He had a big time body, a thick beard—even though he was always clean shaven—full sideburns, and a smile that caused parents and kids, male and female alike, to do double takes. I mean, he was movie star material. When he got up on stage at assembly to make an announcement, everyone stopped whatever he or she was doing and paid attention. It was just natural to admire how perfectly attractive he was.

Like all schools, we also had a vice president, treasurer and secretary, all elected by the students. In our case, they were all female. None of us really knew what they did, but I'm sure the positions were used primarily to embellish their college applications. I had pictures of Masterson making out with each of them. One was out back, behind the athletic center; one was between bookshelves on the second floor of the library; and one, which included his hand underneath her way too short skirt, was in a classroom at night, where they were supposedly studying together. So here he was, getting a taste of all his class officers, and I was in love with a lesbian and had never kissed anyone in my life.

29.

"Hey, Carl."

"Hey, Will."

"Did you do your homework?"

"Some of it."

"How come only some of it?"

"I was kinda busy this week."

"Doing what?"

"Work and stuff."

Eight dollars and seventy-five cents an hour work.

"I thought getting your GED was a priority. Remember? So you can make more money?"

"I know. I kind of fucked up. I'll catch up this week."

"Promise?"

"Yeah."

"I'm going to hold you to that."

"I'll do better. You're a great kid, Will. You're helping me a lot. I don't want to blow this opportunity."

"It's only our fourth class, Carl."

"I know. But I think it's going to work. You're probably the smartest kid I've ever met. And you're a natural teacher."

"Okay, enough praise." Although I kind of liked hearing it. "Let's get down to work. Let's start with our letters."

Once again we pulled out my little brother's old first grade workbook and began our lesson.

I felt good about the progress that Carl and I were making. He would never be mistaken for Hemingway, but we'd gotten through the alphabet and learned to write upper and lower case versions of each letter. His penmanship was no better than a seven year old's, but it was decipherable, and it was progress. And we were beginning to read simple sentences. The old "See Spot run" sequence still worked, even for a thirty-eight year old high school dropout.

While I felt bad for Carl, who had obviously screwed up somewhere in his youth, I saw potential in him. He was small man, maybe six inches shorter than I was, and wiry with heavily calloused hands. When we shook hands, it was likely holding lizard skin. Yet when he shaved and combed his hair, which he did for most of our sessions, he actually could have passed for a banker. Every once in a while, he showed up tired and stubbly. Probably had been out for the night. I would chastise him for that, and he would sheepishly smile. Guilty as charged, he knew.

Over time, he had mentioned he had two young daughters, and I got the sense that neither lived with him. Some days he talked about really wanting to be able to read to his kids. Other times, he didn't say a word about them. I was sure there was a good story there. Maybe someday he would feel comfortable telling me.

30.

As WITH MY FIRST year, basketball season was my salvation. I had basketball, my underground yearbook, and my imaginary romance during the school day with Jelly. And while he drove me crazy most of the time, I even almost looked forward to my sessions with Carl. There was a story there I needed to understand. So while my dad was like the Buckingham Palace guard each night from the time I got home until I went to bed, I had the few things I needed to keep my mind occupied as I sauntered toward growing up. I recognized that I was a relatively uncomplicated person and that I didn't need much.

I made varsity, and while I didn't play a lot, the coach really took to my hustle and toughness. He'd even mentioned in jest a couple of times to the team about my being "the kid who TKO'd Bussmann in the first round." I was making my case for being in the regular rotation as a junior.

Sometimes I wished I'd had my camera at games. Not for the players but for the fans in the bleachers. From my seat near the end of the bench, it was some great people watching. Particularly the Friday night games. Half the adults played the role of proud parents; the other half seethed at the coach because their kids didn't play, or at least not as much as they thought he should let them. It was easy to pick out the kids who had been drinking outside, or, better yet, snuck beer into the game. They were the ones who kept going to the bathroom every five minutes and not coming back for twenty. Their section of the bleachers would get more raucous each time they returned. By the end of the game, they were cheering the timeouts. But the few teachers who came with their young children would never go back to the student section during the game. Too much work for the end of a long school week. This was their time with their own kids.

We were playing one Friday night against one of the many schools that hadn't let me in when I applied. Even at my newfound height, I was still small next to their guys. I was doing my usual cheering gyrations in my warm-up sweats from the bench. I had seen Jelly make a surprise appearance partway through the first half. She wandered toward me as we were trotting off the floor at halftime, heading to the lockers for what was sure to be a hellish speech. We were losing by twenty-one.

"Nice game."

"It's only halftime. What are you doing here?"

"I came to watch the game."

"It's Friday night, so you certainly have better things to do. You don't know anything about basketball."

"Hey, I'm not that dumb. You bounce a rubber ball around, throw it toward a round hole, and if it goes in they give you some points."

"The ball's leather."

"Minor details."

"So what's the real reason you're here?"

"Okay, then I came to watch you play."

"I don't play. I just sit on the bench."

"You have to start somewhere."

It didn't take long to realize her mission. When we came back out for the second half, Jelly was sitting halfway up the center bleacher section—away from the student section. And chatting with my parents.

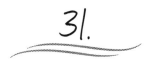

31.

I LIKE VANILLA BETTER than chocolate. I like strawberries and raspberries, but I don't like peaches. I hate peas. Actually I couldn't begin to describe how much I hate peas. From the time I was a little kid, I have always liked hats. Any kind of hat. I like wearing sneakers, and I don't like wearing dress shoes. Summer is my favorite season, but Thanksgiving is my favorite holiday. A little football and a lot of turkey with stuffing and extra gravy. I worry about my grandfather's declining health (he has early stage Alzheimer's). I worry a lot about global warming. I worry about the young men and women not much older than me who are fighting confusing wars in Iraq and Afghanistan. Our president worries me.

I'd been having a dream lately where I would be standing in our backyard and watching myself lie on the ground choking. I couldn't really see the standing me, but the me on the ground was in basic weekend fare of t-shirt and sweats, writhing on the ground, trying to catch my breath. I don't think that the me on the ground was at risk of dying, but he wasn't in a good place by any means.

I really wanted to help. Hell, it was *me* choking on the ground. But as badly as I wanted to help myself, I just couldn't get myself to do anything. All I had to do was reach out my arm. Pull myself up off the ground. Whack myself on the back. Whatever.

But for some reason, I just stood there and watched. I don't know why. I just wouldn't reach out to help.

I'm not a particularly touchy-feely person. And I'm not one who is big on trying to interpret dreams. It was sort of like trying to interpret Mary Shelley or Hemingway. I couldn't do that either. But this dream would come back periodically. I knew it meant something, and I thought I knew what it meant. I was just not sure I wanted to listen.

32.

By the time spring was starting to show hints of appearing, I had mastered academic mediocrity. My grades and teacher comments were consistently uninspiring. My dad's quiet determination to turn me into an intellectual wonder hadn't wavered either. Had to give him credit. I was a tough project, but his was steadfast in this mission to get me going.

I continued to work each Sunday afternoon with Carl. He was frustrating as hell—unfocused, unorganized, completely lacking in discipline. As a result, he didn't make progress as quickly as he should have. In many ways he was like me, and I was playing the role of my dad. Unlike my dad, I sort of enjoyed our sessions. It was a nice feeling to not be the student.

"So how often do you see your daughters?"

"You probably don't want to know, Will."

"How come?"

"You won't think of me as a very nice person."

"I bet you it won't change my view of you."

"I bet it will."

At that point I'd known Carl for four months. We'd meet every Sunday at the town library, and he'd call me on my cell with increasing frequency. Usually it was just to say hello. I think that when his brother wasn't around and he had watched enough television, he would get bored. He didn't have a lot going on in his life. So he would call me. I didn't mind.

I'd sensed the whole time that I had known him that there was a hidden story there, and I was curious as hell to find out what it was. I wouldn't say Carl and I were friends. Hell, he was more than twice my age, illiterate, bagged groceries for a living, and probably wasn't doing much in a good way for society. But somehow we had a small connection. In a weird way, I felt I understood his struggles better than most would, even though I knew very little about him. Maybe he was like me and there was very little to know. I just had to find out.

"Try me."

"I've never seen either of them."

"Huh?"

"I don't even know their names."

"I don't understand."

"I've had relations with some women at the supermarket. There are a lot of single Brazilian women who work there. They come over here to make better money. Eight seventy-five an hour is a pretty good living in Brazil. They don't know very much English, and they don't understand what a real fuckup I am. So they sleep with me because either they're lonely or they think I'm going to lead them to a better life. Two of them have gotten pregnant because of me. Didn't take either long to figure out that there wasn't much to me.

They both went back to their families in Brazil for good before the babies were born."

"How do you know you had daughters?"

"Their Brazilian friends at the store tell me. There is a pretty good pipeline back to their country."

"Aren't you curious to see daughters?"

"Sure. Wouldn't you be?"

"So have you ever thought about going to Brazil to see them?"

"A million times. It's what I dream about every night when I go to bed. But face the facts. I can't buy a ticket online like everyone else because I can't read, and I don't have a credit card. Ditto for a passport. And imagine me trying to find my way through airports to a strange country. I never leave this town because I know my way around it. I can fake it. The few times in my life I've been to Boston, it scared the hell out of me. I had no idea where I was or how I was going to get home. I don't ever want to experience that ever again."

"You're kidding me."

"Scout's honor. I'd do anything to see my daughters. It would be so cool to see if they look like me, to see if we have the same expressions, to see if they hate vegetables like I do. It would be unbelievable if I had these little people who needed me, who loved me, who'd call me daddy. And you know what really scares the hell out of me?"

"What?"

"That I'll go my whole life and they'll never meet me."

I was stunned. This guy bagged groceries and bagged women who couldn't understand a word he said. Yet after making absolutely nothing of his life thus far, he actually really cared about something. He wasn't empty.

"So is that really why you wanted to learn how to read?"

"Yeah. I do need to make more money so I can afford to move to Brazil. But the thought of taking that trip scares me beyond belief. It would be a million times worse than Boston, and I almost crapped in my pants just going to Boston."

"And yet you still want to learn how to read so you can go there?"

"I want to be able to read a bedtime story to my girls."

33.

"So who do you think is the first person that you are going to have sex with?"

"What happened to 'Hi, Will. How are you?'"

"We're past that."

"We are?"

"Yup."

"How do you know I haven't had sex yet?"

"Do you want me to write you a list of reasons?"

"No."

"Okay. So have you at least thought about it?"

I never stopped thinking about it.

"Have you had sex yet?"

"It's different when you like girls."

"How so?"

"We don't have that thing hanging between our legs. There isn't any chance we're going to get knocked up."

"Sounds to me like you ducked the question."

"Pretty clever, huh?

"So are you ever going to come clean and tell me whether you're really a lesbian?"

"I've already told you."

"But I'm not sure I believe you."

"How come?"

"I've never seen you show any romantic interest toward any girl at Pendy."

"You have a fair point."

"And you spend most of your free time with me."

"I can't just hang out and have fun without sleeping with you?"

"Of course you can. But someday you have to answer the question."

34.

Shaky, Jelly and I were hanging out in an empty classroom. It was classic spring weather you get only in New England. Two days of being teased by sun and warm breezes followed by a cold, rainy day that gnaws at you right down to your core. All the afternoon practices had been canceled, so we decided to meet. As opposed to our usual intent to waste time, in this instance we had a mission. I was going to share with my two best friends my recently completed *Pendy According To Will* yearbook.

I had expended more energy on this project than anything I ever had done before. And while I recognized that most would not consider it productive energy, it was energy expended nonetheless. I was kind of proud of my effort to see my secretive yearbook through to completion, as follow through had never been one of my great strengths.

I suppose that in my own way I was trying to figure out how I stacked up against all of the other kids in school. The huge majority of kids at Pendy were richer, smarter, more accomplished, and more confident than me. But I think that I was in some way hoping to find a crack in their apparent perfection. Something that made the ocean between them and me less imposing.

My yearbook had a page on each kid in school. The intent was to capture who they really were. In truth, I knew only very few of them. But through my camera lens—at least I convinced myself of that—I grew to understand them in an entirely different way.

"Better not let Abby see this. You make her look manic depressive. She's cryin' in every picture."

"Greg Masterson is a pig."

"Girls are definitely hotter when they high. They show more skin."

"Dawson's cuter than I thought he was."

"I thought you weren't doing no faculty pictures. Buzzsaw looks like he about to keel over an' croak."

"This is a great picture of Grabow. Put this on her college application and she'll be going to community college."

"Hey, take it easy. That's where I might be going."

"No chance, Shaky. You're smarter than you give yourself credit for."

"Glad someone thinks so."

"Where the hell did you get a picture of the headmaster in a Speedo?"

"Does Fast Eddie ever wear his pants any place except up around his chest?"

"Your pictures of the football coach aren't very flattering."

"I still think Dawson is cute."

"I told you she wasn't a lesbian."

"You make Miss Van Waters seem like such a good person on her page. Kind of like a Superwoman among teachers. How come?"

"You should turn this in for a grade. It is really good."

"My favorite is the page on Moriarity playing with his football."

"Used a little digital adjustment there. Wanted to keep it rated PG."

"Actually looks like a big adjustment."

"You'd get a 'A.'"

"Never seen this kid before."

"Or maybe an 'F' and they would kick me out."

"I actually look pretty fine in my pictures."

"Hey, how come there's only a black and white computer outline on my page?"

Maybe I wasn't quite as far away from the rest as I thought. At least I would have liked to have believed that.

35.

WILL WOULD TELL HIS *friends whenever we punished him. I had gained the reputation of being the strictest parent at Pendy. It didn't bother me. I wasn't going to let my kid waste his natural ability sneaking out drinking in the middle of the night. I know Will never would have even thought to do that on his own. Nonetheless, he knew better.*

He seemed to be doing better since his latest grounding. But with Will, progress too often seemed to be temporary. He could crank it up for a day, a week, or a month. To date, staying focused for a full term had proven to be far too elusive for him. I was prepared to do whatever it took to get him on the right track and to get him to begin to realize his God given talent. But babysitting him every night was no longer enough.

I tried to pretend to both my wife and myself that I was just giving Will helpful pointers on his projects and writing assignments. But we both knew I was doing way more than that. Sometimes when it was late and he was far behind, I would just grab the keyboard and basically write a whole paper for him. It was our way of keeping up with his classmates. We almost never discussed it, but Amy, Will, and I all knew what was happening. I went to work each morning and did my job. When I came home at night I was essentially doing my sophomore year in high school all over again—algebra, US history, chemistry, American lit, and

Spanish. It was fatiguing, and I knew it was wrong. I just wasn't going to let my kid fall any further behind.

As parents, we all worried about how our kids stacked up against their peers and whether or not they were going to get into a good college. It was like we held our breath through all of their games, events, and report cards from the time they entered first grade, always hopeful there would arrive a time when they would be accepted at an elite school and we could finally exhale. We never talked about it with our friends because, in reality, we were competing with each other. But all of us were quite familiar with the feeling.

Somebody once told me that the measure of success of a man is not how great an athlete he was in high school, how many women he slept with in college, or how big his bank account was as an adult. He said that the true measure of a man was how many people attended his funeral. Given that I was beginning in so many ways to cross the line of being a good father to Will, I really expected that mine might well be a small gathering. And even though I was justifying my actions as providing help to Will, I'm not sure he would come to the funeral either.

36.

My recurring dream took a new twist.

It started off the way it always did. I would be walking down a street and see a person lying on his back, gasping for air and choking on something he couldn't expel from his throat. While the person looked less and less like me, I knew it was me. And for the countless time, I did nothing to help.

Only this time, as I stood watching, Dawson would come out of nowhere and calmly walk over to where I was choking. He was dressed neatly in his dress shoes and blue blazer, with his Windsor knot covering the top button of his pressed shirt. He calmly stooped down and pulled me to a seated position before giving me several kind but firm hits to the back until I coughed up whatever object was stuck in my throat. He stood up, looked at the original me standing on the sidelines and gave me a knowing wink before he walked out of my sight.

I had no idea what he was doing in my dream.

CLASS II

37.

"So what are you going to do you about college?"

"I try not to think about it too much."

"You're going to go, aren't you?"

"I suppose."

"You don't sound thrilled by the idea."

Jelly and I were lying on the grassy hill behind the Fort. It was an Indian summer day in early October. The leaves were already changing, but it nonetheless felt like July. We were both skipping cross-country practice because the weather was too nice. We'd pay for it at some point, but that point seemed too far away at that moment to worry about.

I was usually never one to appreciate things like the weather, but it was truly an amazing day. Lying on our backs, hands folded behind our heads, there was nothing but blue before us. It was the kind of day that put a smile on everyone's face. It wasn't a traditional robin's egg blue; in fact, it was almost transparent. A beautiful oasis of sky. They wouldn't have it in any paint swatch book or on the computer. Maybe I just liked it because I was alone with Jelly. But whatever the reason, I wished that I had my camera. I would have liked to capture this blue and store it for my own memory.

Jelly's new fashion style my junior year was to not shave her armpits. Hairy armpits were not one of my favorite looks for girls, but as with everything else she was able to pull it off. With her arms stretched behind her head and wearing her familiar tank top, her hollows were in full view. A slight hint of red on her now brown hair, a rare occasion when her true colors showed.

"I don't really like school."

"Don't you think college will be better? More freedom. Stay up late, sleep late. Take the classes you want to take. Living on your own."

"Yeah, but my sense is that you gotta work pretty hard. Way harder than high school, which, as we both know, is proving to be a pretty good stretch for me."

"I'm looking forward to it."

"Really?"

"This place is too small. Everybody is the same. Except for you, of course."

"I'm not that different."

"In your own special way, you are. Everyone here is so fixated on getting drunk, getting laid, getting nice cars for their birthdays, and sucking up to teachers so they can get good recommendations for college. It's pretty pathetic."

"Yeah, they could be like me instead. Fixated on nothing."

"That's not true."

"Nice try, but it kind of is true. I mean, I don't really want to do anything except chill. I don't feel any desire … any need … to prepare myself for some arbitrary time down the road which I don't feel will ever come."

"Why? Are you planning to do something dramatic, like blow your brains out?"

"No. Nothing like that. Besides, it would be too much work. Plus I wouldn't want to leave a mess for anybody to have to clean up."

She laughed.

"It all just seems such a long way off," I said blandly, maybe talking as much to myself as I was to Jelly.

"It's probably closer than you think."

"You sound like my father."

"I didn't think my voice was that deep."

"Actually, his isn't deep at all. Sometimes when telemarketing people randomly call our house, they call him 'ma'am.' It really pisses him off. So how many colleges are you applying to?"

"Sixteen. Although I may decide to apply to one early decision."

"That sounds like a lot."

"I think most kids here apply to that many."

"Do you know which one you want to go to?"

"I'm not really sure yet. I just know I want to get as far away from home as I can."

"So you can get away from me?"

"Of course."

"Thought so."

"So you want to go up to my room?"

"Huh?"

A shiver ran the full length of my body. A mixture of surprise, exhilaration, and unbridled fear.

"My room!"

"I can't."

"Why not?"

"I'm not allowed."

"Don't be so chicken."

"I don't want to get kicked out of here."

"I thought you didn't like it here that much."

"It's still a better alternative to getting expelled."

"It could be fun."

"What would we do?"

"Who knows? We could figure something out."

"It sounds like one of your bad ideas."

"Third floor. Last room on the left. By the fire escape."

I knew where it was.

"How would I get up there?"

"You're smart. Figure it out."

"I was afraid you were going to say that."

Jelly got up and jogged off to the stairs that wound up to the back entrance of the Fort. Her legs moved in a natural symmetry; her hair bobbed side to side with each stride. For a total nonathlete she actually ran pretty well. She probably could have been pretty decent on the playing fields, but this was just another way for her to buck convention.

To prevent such activities as we were now contemplating, the dorm rooms on the Fort were separated—boys on the second floor, girls on the third. The faculty dorm parents on each floor tried to create an intimate atmosphere for the boarders. They would invite the students living on their floors in for hot chocolate study breaks or for movies and popcorn on weekends. The boarders, even Jelly, seemed to like being part of the tight-knit group. It was one of Pendy's better features.

And here I was skipping practice and figuring out how to scale the family fortress.

Reluctantly, I got up and started to walk toward the Fort after her, not having any idea how the hell I was going to get up to her room.

38.

"YOU'RE SHAKING."

"It was kind of exciting."

"How did you get up here?"

"You don't want to know."

"Yes I do."

"I'll tell you later after I stop shaking."

"You'd better."

"So what do we do now?"

"How about a drink?"

"You have booze up here?"

"No. I just thought I'd get a reaction out of you."

"It worked."

"So how did you get up here?"

"Man, you don't ever give up, do you?"

"I told you before that it's one of my better qualities."

"We'll have to have a discussion about that someday."

The rooms were small—I could just about touch the two walls if I reached out my arms. Two basic mattresses on two simple wooden frames and two matching dressers that had drawers on one side and a place to hang clothes on the other. In the corner farthest from the door were two utilitarian desks with utilitarian lamps and wooden chairs. This is where I had seen her study at night through my camera lens.

Like her car, the room could have used a massive cleanup. The bed wasn't made. Clothes and other crap were piled everywhere—on the bed, the dresser, the floor. It reminded me of one of those Jackson Pollack paintings that they had shown in art class sophomore year. Lots of color, but not a lot of purpose. Somehow I'd known it would look like this.

The one surprise was that her desk was perfectly organized. On the left hand side were four textbooks. The largest book, *Fundamentals of Physics*, was on the bottom, and then, mounted in order of size, came calculus, European history and French. All were facing the same direction. Next to the stack of textbooks was a smaller pile of novels, all of which were American classics. *Catch 22, For Whom The Bell Tolls, The Great Gatsby, Babbitt, Long Day's Journey Into Night*. Even I had heard of most of these. Each of the novels was heavily dog-eared. On the right corner of the desk sat five large spiral notebooks, one obviously for each subject she took. There were no scribbles, notes of boredom or cartoons like those that decorated my notebooks. In the middle of her desk sat her daily planner opened to today's date. She had extremely neat handwriting.

Still, there I stood, shaking with fear and anticipation. There was no place I would rather have been at that very moment.

"There is a closed off stairway in the turret by the loading dock," I began to explain. "Shaky showed me it one time. It's actually pretty cool. It leads up to this empty attic at the very top that's full of old newspapers—and it has a great view of Boston. I remembered him saying that there was a door on this floor that let you into the back of the janitor's closet. I just let myself in."

"Shaky lets himself onto the girls' floor?"

"He once told me that Jessie Grabow sleeps with shit all over her face."

"Figures."

"I've only taken pictures of her."

"Stuck up bitch."

"So I shouldn't ask her out?"

"That's your call. How come you have never taken me up to the turret?"

"No reason. It's really Shaky's discovery. I just go hang with him sometimes. I like reading the old newspapers."

"Will you bring me up there sometime?"

"Sure, if I survive this excursion."

"Still worried?"

"Yes."

"You've stopped shaking."

"I'm sure I could start up again if you want."

"No. I don't want to add any more stress to your already high anxiety life. But enough small talk. How about we get naked?"

"Was that just for reaction too?"

"No. That was serious."

"Naked?"

"You have seen me naked before."

"No I haven't."

"Sure you have. In your mind, anyway, you've at least *imagined* me naked before." She placed her finger on my temple and twisted it like a screwdriver. I didn't say anything because she was right. "Last year when I called you in the buff. And probably every night after that for a week."

I still didn't say anything. It had been much longer than a week.

"I'm right, aren't I." It was more of a statement than a question. "And besides, you are pretty obvious when you try to look at my boobs when I bend over."

"How come you have never said anything?"

"I think it's kind of flattering. Besides, you're a growing boy. You need some stimulation."

"You always know how to say the right things."

"So what do you think?"

The thought of seeing her naked was incredible. I couldn't think of anything I'd have liked more. I also knew that I would be expelled if we were caught. And my father would kill me. But at this moment that mattered less to me than it usually did. Jelly was an avowed lesbian who was possibly going to step into a straight person's world. Maybe she was just teasing me. Or maybe she was testing herself. Again, at that moment it didn't really matter. Either way I was elated.

But per my usual luck, voices began to be heard from the hallway on the floors below. Kids returning early from the afternoon practices. The clacking of cleats on the linoleum tile was familiar to all of us at the school. And one of them would be Jelly's roommate.

"Damn. I gotta go."

"You're going to miss the show."

"I know. But I want to keep my life as it is. Can I take a rain check?"

"You're shaking again."

"That's because I'm scared shitless."

"Can you get out okay?"

"I think so. But I really gotta go."

And I turned to go, realizing that I was about to miss the greatest moment of my life to date. Par for the course, unfortunately.

"Hey."

"Whaaaat?" I loudly whispered.

I looked back quickly; she'd pulled down her shirt strap to reveal her left breast. I can only imagine the look that was on my face. She just stood there, temporarily revealing, and laughed. Finally I dashed out.

All the way home that night and for days beyond, I had only a single picture in my mind. It was some great sight.

39.

I DIDN'T SEE JELLY for more than a week after the dorm incident. I seemed to keep missing her in the hallways and at lunch, and she was absent from cross-country practice. At first I thought she might have been a little embarrassed. But Jelly didn't embarrass easily. I later learned she was doing college visits.

Nonetheless, I was on a bit of a roll. A few days later, I made out with Abby. I don't know why or exactly how it happened, but we just made out. Our team had a Saturday cross-country meet. It was a nice day, and I'd done pretty well. So all in all, I was feeling reasonably good. One of the jobs of the runners on the home team was to collect the signs on the running trail that pointed out the directions in the woods where we ran. Abby had come to watch some of the games that Saturday and decided to join me as I walked through the woods picking up the signs. The next thing I knew we were making out. I had never really kissed anyone before and probably wasn't any good at it. Abby, in fact, seemed a lot better at it than me. But I wasn't worried at all. It wasn't like I was going to date Abby or anything. So there was no stress involved.

40.

So much of the conversation junior year centered around the college process. We had to meet with our newly assigned college counselors every few weeks to create a target list of where we wanted to go to school. Coming up with far reach, reach, achievable, and safety schools become part of all the meetings. The way I looked at it, all the colleges were a reach for me. The difference between applying to prep school and applying to college was that rather than my parents, I now had a professional to write essays for me.

In October we had to take the PSATs. These were the practice for the standardized tests required to get into most colleges. Many of the kids—usually those with the most expensive cars in the school parking lot—actually paid for practice courses or individualized tutors for the PSAT. Tutors for the practice test—that really blew me away.

The tests were on a Saturday morning and started earlier than I usually awoke on weekends. I brought enough #2 pencils to write the Torah but not enough learning to get a great score. They had taped thick brown paper over the entire basketball court so we wouldn't scratch it and had placed desks that had the chair and writing platform attached in even rows across the court. The whole stressed-out junior class would spend four hours together in the gym sweating out the test. Now that I had grown to a full six foot four, the desks didn't actually fit me that well. I was sure my back would be all knotted up by the time the test was over.

What was interesting was that the usual fission that occurred each morning at assembly was not there for the exam. Each kid seemed lost in his or her own little thought world trying to remember the lessons from the tutors or the last SAT words that had been drilled into his or her head over the past two and a half years. It was almost as if this group of a hundred kids didn't really know each other anymore. I said good morning to Abby, who I'd made out with just a week before, and got only an empty glance back.

I certainly seemed to be missing the purpose of this whole practice event.

41.

As the first term moved along, Shaky and I had been spending more time in the Fort turret. We'd read the bulk of the old newspapers so there wasn't as much to do up there. Sometimes we'd play cards—crazy eights, rummy, once in a while a little Texas Hold'em. But mostly I think we were just escaping thinking about college. By that time the reality of a future after high school was beginning to set in for all of us. It was what everyone was talking about, but it was a step that neither of us wanted to take.

"So you think we can just stay up here for four years instead of going to college?"

"It would be a lot cheaper."

"I'll say."

"You could take your pictures, an' I could sleep."

"For four years?"

"It's what they call hibernating. Don't your remember science class in ninth grade?"

"How could I forget? Are you going to college?"

"Yeah, I'll go somewhere. I really don't care where."

"Think you'll get in? Our grades aren't the best, you know."

"Yeah, but I'm poor an' black. They like that. Feel like they saving the world by letting kids like me in. I'm guessing I'll have a few choices, and they'll pay for the whole thing. Just like here. I'll coast by for another four, come out with a nice degree, and not really know very much worthwhile about anything 'cept the lessons I learnt in my neighborhood."

"So if you get out of college and get a job and make some money, will you stay in your neighborhood, or will you move out to someplace safe?"

"You mean like a town like this one with lots of grass and trees?"

"I guess."

"I love grass and trees. And I'd move as far away from my neighborhood as I could. California may be too close."

"Really?"

"Think about it. That neighborhood took my parents. My grandma lives afraid all the time. And most the kids have done drugs by high school. I may not get the best grades, but I ain't stupid."

"You going to leave your grandmother alone?"

Shaky slumped back against the wall. He had obviously thought about this before.

"It's my biggest worry. She won't want to go. Dorchester is all she knows."

I guessed we all had our own unique worries.

42.

"You want to go with me to the Christmas semi-formal?"

"Me?"

"Somebody already ask you?"

"Me? Hardly."

"The lesbian excuse again."

"Works pretty well, don't you think?"

"You're going to have to tell me someday if it really is true."

"Why? Are you interested in going out with me?"

"Probably."

"How romantic."

"I'm doing my best, given my limited practice."

"All you have to do is see my breasts and all of a sudden you want to date me? You're just like all the boys."

"Remember, I only saw one breast."

"I didn't know you were counting."

"I can certainly count to two."

The Christmas semi-formal was a longstanding tradition at Pendy. They had been doing it forever, beginning way back when the school was in Boston. It was supposedly an incredibly festive event that only juniors and seniors were allowed to attend. Everyone came in their best formal attire—fancy gowns for the girls and suits or tuxedos for the guys. All of the faculty came as well, and apparently they let their guards down a little bit. It was supposed to be a social interaction where staff and students interacted as peers for the first time. A sign there was hope for all of us growing up.

My real mission was to try to figure out if Jelly had been keeping a little secret. After our almost incident in her room in the Fort, I was beginning to believe that her lesbian claim was a façade. It was her way to be different, her way to stay in control of her relationships, her way to keep an emotional balance in her life. By telling everyone that she liked girls, she wouldn't have to get caught up falling for the Greg Mastersons of the world. On the other hand, maybe I still just wanted to believe that for my own selfish reasons. But I was hoping this more formal date might provide me with the opportunity to get some clarity.

"You're getting so grown up. What happened to the naïve little boy with the nice ass?"

"He's growing up."

"Not too much, I hope."

"No, not too much."

"I like your mustache."

"Are you making fun of me?"

"Just a little. Have you shaved yet?"

"Once."

"How soon till the next one?"

"Probably a while. I wasn't as momentous as I thought."

"I hear you. I never shave my armpits anymore."

"I've noticed."

"Or my legs."

"I've noticed that too."

"Man, you don't miss much, do you?"

"The blonde hair on your legs is hard to see. No one can tell you haven't shaved them."

"Think that will hurt my image?"

"Not much is going to hurt your image."

I didn't really shave yet, but I towered over Jelly. I liked the fact that she now had to look up to me when we talked. And I wasn't necessarily eye candy yet, as I was still pretty damned skinny. But it was becoming clear to me that there was potential.

"So you really want to take me to the prom?"

"It's a semi-formal."

"And you know the difference?"

"Not really."

"What about Abby?"

"I'm asking you."

"She's a lot richer than I am."

"I'll have to live with that."

"Okay then."

"Good."

"You going to pick me up?"

"You live upstairs from the party."

"You didn't answer my question."

"I'll drive you home."

43.

"Hey, Will."

"Hey, Dawson."

"Can I ask you something?"

"Sure."

Since our time together doing tech theater freshman year, Dawson and I had formed a unique sort of connection. I wouldn't call it a friendship, but there was at least a mutual respect there—created by one early conversation during which we actually opened up a little to each other. So during assembly, when Abby was talking our ear off, we actually would have small, unsubstantial discussions. I rarely saw him after assembly as he was in all the smart kid classes and no longer ran cross-country. When I saw him in the hallway, it was somewhat of a surprise—almost like he had been looking for me. But it was Friday at the end of the day. I was in no rush to do much of anything.

We were in the Main School, and he had waved me over to an alcove off the primary thruway to the auditorium.

He gulped. I never in my life made anyone nervous except Dawson.

"Are you seeing anyone?"

"No."

"You're not?"

"I think I'd know." Again, when I wasn't feeling like I was on stage, I could be a wiseass.

He smiled a sort of wicked smile that I hadn't ever seen on him before. I'm not sure I realized the significance of the unusual smile until many months later. But wicked was definitely the right word to describe it.

"Do you think you might be interested in going to the semi-formal with me?"

I think I was too surprised to be stunned.

"Huh?"

"I thought there might be a chance you're gay like me."

"You're gay?"

"You hadn't figured it out?"

"I can be a little slow on the uptake."

"So you're not gay?"

"I don't think so."

"I thought your relationship with Jelly was a little different. So I just sort of assumed you were."

"Believe it or not, I can actually understand that. How'd you know you were gay?"

"I've liked boys as long as I can remember. My parents have suspected it forever but have never admitted it. They try their best to convince me that I'm not without ever mentioning it."

"Doesn't sound like fun."

"It's against our religion. As you know, we're Mormon. My father is a bishop in our church, which is a pretty big deal. Being gay is a sin in our church. Basically they expel you if they can't convert you. Would be bad news to expel the son of the bishop."

"Sort of like Rudolph covering up his red nose."

"Never thought of it that way. But it's a fair analogy."

So Dawson was gay, and his parents would kill him if word got out.

"Aren't your parents going to bury you if you show up at the dance with a guy for a date?"

"I'm sure they are. But I've had enough. I can't go on being Rudolph. It's killing me."

"So I'm the first guy you've ever asked out?"

"Yeah. I really didn't mean to embarrass you."

"Don't worry about it. I've had a kind of rough few years overall. I think I'm pretty oblivious to being embarrassed."

And I think I meant that. Strangely, I wasn't bothered that Dawson had thought I was gay. I think I was comfortable that I wasn't. But what I liked was that I finally had a little insight into this mannequin I had been sitting next to for two and a half years. He rarely spoke because he was petrified. Petrified about his own sexuality. Petrified that he had a crush on the guy he sat next to each morning.

"So why me?"

He looked straight at me. Not over my head or at his feet. He knew the answer.

"You're not overpowering like most guys. You don't walk around like you have a football in your crotch and testosterone oozing out of your pores. You have a cuteness to you."

"A cuteness?"

"If I used a different word I'd be lying."

At that point I wasn't sure I felt so good about the conversation anymore. I hadn't been aiming for cute.

When I came in Monday morning, Dawson wasn't there. What was strange was that Dawson never missed school. As long as I had known him, he'd never been sick or skipped assembly. He may have been a strange kid, but I think that school was still his refuge from a home life where he fit in even less. So for the first time the seat to my left was empty.

I wondered if this had something to do with him being in my dream.

44.

"WILL, THANKS FOR STOPPING by."

"Sure, Coach. What's up?"

Coach's little office was a pigsty. My bedroom may have been better. The legend was that the reason he was always so late in getting corrected papers back to the kids was that he'd lost them in his office. I'd never had him as a teacher, though.

"I've been very pleased with the way you have been playing this year. You've stepped it up a lot from last season."

"Thanks, Coach."

"And your length is really making a difference for you. You can really shoot over kids this year."

"Thanks again, Coach."

"But I'm taking you out of the starting lineup."

"I thought you said I've been playing well."

"You have been. But Justin is playing better."

"He's only a freshman!"

"Doesn't make a difference. The guy who is contributing most plays the most. That's always been my policy. You'll still play, but you'll be coming off the bench."

"This sucks, Coach."

"Just keep working hard. You're a valuable member of the team."

"It still sucks, Coach."

And so again I couldn't catch a break. The one thing I cared about at Pendy. It was the one area in which I'd truly worked hard to earn my spot, and the coach was going to give it to a new recruit.

"I got demoted."

"To Class III?"

"No. Out of the starting lineup."

"It's only a dumb sport."

I couldn't believe Jelly was becoming my sports confidant. She cared less about sports that just about anyone I knew.

"Not to me. It's the only thing at this school I care about."

"Thanks."

"You know what I mean."

"You'll be fine."

"I got beat out by a freshman."

"Don't worry about it. Your father won't kill you."

"You never know."

"Well I, at least, have some good news."

"What's that?"

"I got accepted to Princeton, early decision."

"Princeton?"

"Uh huh."

"That's incredible."

"You sound surprised."

"I actually didn't know you were that good of a student."

"You should know by now that I am full of surprises."

"Is that where you want to go?"

"That would be why I applied early decision."

"Ivy League."

"Weird, huh?"

"I'm really happy for you."

"Are you?"

"Yeah, I am. It's just a little scary."

"How so?"

"In three years, I don't think I've ever even seen you study." I lied a little about that. "You don't do all the usual activities and suck up to teachers to pad your record. And you got into Princeton. I figure I'm a dead man. Who the hell would want to let me go to their college?"

"Don't be so hard on yourself."

"Maybe I could just join the army."

"Then I'd be afraid for our national defense."

"Me too."

"I think we should go out and celebrate."

"It's been a while since I've played miniature golf."

We both smiled at each other.

45.

"Hi, Will."

"Hey, Abby."

"Did you guys win yesterday?"

"Uh huh."

"Cool."

"I guess."

"How many points did you have?"

"Eleven."

"So that's pretty good."

"For a kid who used to start."

Making out or no making out, Abby remained the one straight girl in my life who ever actually liked me. And I had to give her credit; she was determined. She really was a nice person, but there was nothing there. I knew where this conversation was going to go, and it wasn't within my limited comfort zone. Abby was like one of the guys. She knew a lot about sports and cursed more than anyone I knew. She was also really rich. She drove a new silver BMW to school.

"Can I ask you a question?"

"Sure."

She was turning red. This wasn't going to be good.

"Do you want to go to the semi-formal with me?"

"Really?"

"Yeah, really."

She was clearly a little excited by my response. I probably didn't use the right line. As we were juniors and this was our first Christmas semi-formal, there was a certain amount of pressure to get a date, particularly getting one before all the good kids were used up. If that didn't work, you could always invite a kid from some other school, but that apparently never went very well since they didn't really know anyone else at our school. It was our first chance to pretend we were grown up, so getting the basics right early—like a decent date—was important.

"I'm sorry. I can't."

"Oh."

"I don't want to seem mean or anything, but I'm already going with someone else."

"You are?"

"Is it that surprising?"

"It's just that I kind of asked around, and everyone seemed to think you weren't going."

"I guess I can understand that."

"Who are you going with?"

"Jelly."

"Isn't she a lesbian?"

"So she says."

"What, are you going to try to cure her?"

"I've been asked that before, but I don't think that's possible."

"Are you sure?"

"No. But I'm sorry if I disappointed you. I really am flattered you asked me."

"Do you like Jelly?"

"You mean like romantically?"

"Yeah."

I paused because I knew what the answer was but I wasn't prepared yet to admit it.

"I'm not really sure."

"Might be kind of a tough relationship."

"I'll say."

So I was going to go to the dance with a lesbian after having turned down a proposal from a guy. And I was actually turning down the one person I actually could have, at least in theory, dated. You just can't make this stuff up.

46.

"So you know what you want?"

"I think I'm going to have The Ultimate Bertucci."

"What the heck is that?"

"Pizza with sausage, hamburger, chicken, ham and extra cheese, all in one."

"Individual size?"

"No, large."

"You can finish all that?"

"I'll bring the leftovers home for a snack."

"Unbelievable."

"Thanks, Dad, for bringing me."

"You're welcome. I wanted to talk to you about something."

"College?"

"Yeah."

"My college counselor says you guys should leave us alone and let us work through the process with her."

"You've known your college counselor for a month."

"It's what she does."

"I've known you for seventeen years."

"So go ahead."

"Are you planning to visit any colleges during spring break?"

"I dunno. I hadn't thought about it yet."

"Well maybe you should. I figure we have about fifteen hundred miles of driving ahead of us."

"I'll take that bet."

"Trust me. We have to go to Maine to see Colby and Bowdoin. We might as well see Bates while we're there. Then we have to go to Connecticut to see Connecticut College. We probably should add Trinity and Yale. Then we have to do New York and Pennsylvania. Hamilton, Union, Haverford, Swarthmore."

"Yale?"

"What's wrong with that?"

"I could never get in."

"You never know until you try."

"Have you seen my PSAT scores?"

"You're getting tutored. Your scores will rise."

"How about my grades?"

"It's worth the shot."

"Dad, I'm not smart enough to go there. I'd get killed in class."

"Don't sell yourself short."

"Can we change the subject?"

"Not just yet. What else are you planning to do this summer?"

"I was going to be a counselor at basketball camp again."

"You need something to show that you're well rounded."

"But I'm not that well rounded."

"How about a homeless shelter?"

"I prefer where I currently live."

"Serving meals there, Einstein, not living there."

"I'll think about it."

"That's what you always say."

"Can we change the subject again?"

47.

The Fort attic was becoming our oasis. Shaky and I would sneak up there when it got dark and no one could see us enter the cove, the secret passage to our safe haven. We could sit up there and waste time in record proportions. But we didn't care. We were free from homework and parents and college applications and all the other stresses that made up our everyday lives.

With our stacks of old newspapers we discovered our own history without textbooks and pop quizzes. Neither of us would get a bad grade that might hurt our diminishing chances of getting into a great college. Our guardians' dream.

Tonight we brought a little extra class to the attic as we were decked out for the semi-formal. I, of course, wore my usual blue blazer and khaki pants. Shaky, even though he didn't have a date and didn't seem to care, wore a full tux. He slept on his grandmother's couch in a housing project but wore a tux to the dance. The ultimate contradiction.

Jelly looked sensational. Even Shaky noticed. I had never seen her dressed up before. It was not the three hundred dollar dress that everyone else would wear. It looked more like she had gone shopping at the Salvation Army. And she naturally hadn't shopped for a bra.

But her hair was pulled back, and, for the first time since I met her, she was wearing makeup. Almost like a very classy hooker. But I say that as the supreme compliment.

"I didn't know you smoked."

"There are still lots of things you don't know about me."

"When did you start smoking?"

"I never did."

"Then why are you smoking now?"

"It's a character flaw."

"Can I bum one offa ya?" The tuxedo-clad Shaky had joined in.

"Shaky, you smoke too?"

"Look at me, man. I put anything and everything into my body. No holding back now."

"You want one?"

"Nah. I hate cigarette smoke."

Jelly exhaled into my face.

"Thanks."

"Oh, I forgot. You're the jock. Don't want to damage those beautiful lungs."

"Nice try. But you can't make me blush anymore."

"Wanna bet?"

"Not really."

"So who wants wine?" Jelly proceeded to whip out a bottle of wine and a picnic blanket from the oversized bag she was carrying, along with a corkscrew. "Both of your parents think you're at the school dance. It's Friday night. We've got a few hours ahead of us."

"Now we're talking, girl. I already tol' you. I put anything in my body."

"How often do you drink?"

"Whenever I can. In my neighborhood you take advantage of every chance you kin get to forget what's around you."

"Really?"

"Come stay at my apartment some night with me and my grandma. You'll see. It's scary, but it's home."

"How 'bout you, cutey boy? You going to join us?"

"Why not? Guess it can't hurt too much."

"Willdog, you ever drink before?"

Jelly laughed her knowing laugh.

"Yeah, once. Didn't go over too well."

Jelly kept laughing even more.

"Sounds like I'm missing somethin' here."

"I took cutey boy out drinking one time. He had two beers and spent the rest of the night barfing his brains out. His parents grounded him for three months."

"Heh, heh, heh. Way to go, Willdog. You growing up."

"Better than throwing up."

"Just go slow and you'll be fine. Wine's got a nasty kick if you go too fast."

We sat quietly for a while, nursing our wine, and the two of them sucking on their cigarettes. The stone walls were so thick that we could have been having a blowout party and no one would have heard. Same would have been true if we'd shot each other.

"This be nice. It's so very calm."

"I think I'm getting a buzz."

"You're only halfway through your first cup."

"I'm new at this, remember?"

These were the two closest friends I had in the world. One I knew I would never see again once we graduated and went our separate ways. The other I was irreparably in love with—something I think we both knew. But it seemed that nothing would ever happen. It was like three years of Chinese water torture. But they kept me sane and kept me entertained. So I guessed I could live with that.

Jelly all at once broke the calm and jumped up from where she was sitting.

"Okay, who wants to dance?"

"Shaky," I responded out of a strong sense of self-preservation.

"There ain't no music."

"Willy, you sing."

"Hardly."

Jelly was already up dancing to music playing only in her head. I had to admire what I saw. I had pictured her naked in my mind many times, beginning with the first cell phone call. I had seen one of her breasts. I'd felt her loose, hanging boobs many times as she brushed up against me in the hallway in school—sometimes accidentally and sometimes trying to get a rise out of me. She was bouncing all over the place now, but she'd gotten used to my watching her.

We all began to drink faster than we should have. But the setting was relaxing, even surreal. All of the worries of our respective worlds were a million miles away. And the alcohol went down smoothly. It just felt good.

Shaky lifted his massive bulk and began to gyrate with her. It took only a few twists for him to begin to perspire. Her arms above her head, eyes closed, the lit cigarette dangling from her lips. Shaky weaving and heaving, wine in one hand, cancer stick in the other, lips pursed as he too began to hear Jelly's imagined music.

"You can dance, girl. How come I ain't ever seen you boogie before?"

"I'm shy. Haven't you noticed?"

"Girl, if you shy, then I'm skinny."

"Welcome to my world, Toothpick."

Just as she could reel me into her world, she could suck Shaky into hers too. He grabbed her hands and began to twirl her like he had been dancing his whole life.

"Ever kiss a lesbian?"

"Nope. But I'm ready to try."

And with that she leaned forward and gave Shaky a brief but tongue-spiked kiss, looking at me out of the corner of her eye as she did. I was instantly jealous. After three years, I hadn't gotten even a peck.

"Looks like three's a crowd."

The booze made me more clever than usual.

"Don't worry, Willdog. My grandma don't let me date girls whose hair changes color all the time. She's still your girl. I'm just breakin' her in."

"She's not my girl."

"Sure she is. You two just ain't figured it out yet."

And with that a flame shot out from the back of the *Boston Globe* stacks. Big and orange and hot. It was more than startling to three buzzed, unaware teenagers in their best clothes. Jelly's cigarette was missing, and she hadn't realized it. It had obviously been thrown from her lips during one of Shaky's twirls. And although it was initially a small flame, it wasn't going away by itself.

"Oh shit," stammered Shaky. "Let's get the fuck outta here."

His huge frame bolted for the stairs as fast as his massive legs would take him, swinging open the old metal door at the top of the stairs and using the rails for all the support they could muster as he raced half drunk to obscurity.

Jelly turned and looked at me, the flames already beginning to shoot above her head. Her frozen stare stopped me in my tracks. She looked but didn't say a thing. She was totally sober. To my surprise, she turned back to pick up her bag and then turned to the door to follow Shaky.

I remained frozen. Though I knew I could flee and probably save my soul, I somehow couldn't go. I couldn't let this old building burn. It had lasted too many years. It didn't deserve to end its reign because of the stupidity of a few misguided teenagers.

I grabbed our blanket and began to fan the flames, only to see the blanket quickly catch fire as well. The heat was growing with the flames, and I was conscious that I was starting to sweat badly.

I remembered from my foray in the fall to Jelly's room that there were fire extinguishers in the hallway on her floor. Faster than I had ever before in my life, I flew down the stairs and threw open the door first to the back of the janitor's closet and then to the hallway of the girls' floor. The second door created a huge crash as it slammed into the wall behind. As I ran down the hall toward where I remembered the fire extinguishers were, a couple of underclass girls who were not at the dance popped their heads out of their rooms into the hallway, wondering, I was sure, what the huge crash had been. To their surprise they saw the maddened dash of a schoolmate they probably vaguely recognized with a crazed look on his face and sweat pouring down his neck and shirt.

I easily found two canisters, grabbed them, and began to work my way back to the attic. The smoke had started to pour from the now open hallway door. Soon the fire alarms would sound. I raced back to the stairs with the two filled barrels weighing far more than I had anticipated. Though now over six foot four, I was still not particularly strong and the dual weights caused a struggle as I wrestled the tin drums up the curving stairs.

By the time I reached the top, my head was pounding from the combination of the fear and the alcohol, my shoulders burned from the weight of the fire extinguishers, and my eyes stung from sweat and smoke. I pointed the small hose blindly in what I sensed was the direction of the fire and squeezed the grip with all my strength. White foam exploded out of the hose, an unexpected jolt knocking me backward to the point I almost toppled down the stairs. Regaining my balance, I pushed forward toward the flames, my arm extended as far as it could as if the added stretch would better protect me from the heat.

The foam seemed to make a little dent in the fire, but as the extinguisher exhausted itself, the flames regenerated just as fast as they had dissipated. I was conscious that my breathing was becoming increasingly difficult and that far off there was a loud staccato noise, certainly the fire alarms awakening the courage of the great old building. I reached for the second canister, my fingers quickly pulling back from the burn of the now white hot metal cylinder. With little other choice, I peeled off my shirt to become an oven mitt and picked up my only weapon, again blowing out the white foam to fight a hopeless fight.

The noise from below was increasing, but I was having a hard time concentrating on exactly what and where it was coming from. The old newspapers were creating an incinerator; I was going to become only more fuel. But I couldn't sacrifice the Fort. It was the heart of the school.

I staggered back toward the stairs, or maybe I was already down on the third landing. I couldn't quite remember. It was getting very hard to see. I was feeling my way along the wall. I remember falling a couple of times, tripping over the emptied canisters or the curved stairs or something. My eyes hurt like hell. I couldn't open them anymore.

THE NEXT THING I remember I was resting on a bench outside behind the Fort wearing a Pendy sweatshirt that didn't belong to me. Mr. Sanders, the headmaster, and my mother and father were there, so I knew it couldn't be good.

I looked up at the turret that housed our oasis. I was stunned by how much damage there was. Remains of smoke still floated up through a roof that was no more. The few enduring tiles were charred black, and a section of the huge stones that directly supported the turret roof showed massive burn scars.

Two fire engines and more firemen than I could count at that moment occupied the pavement between where I sat and the entrance to the Fort. I was dizzy.

"How are you feeling?"

"Good."

"Good?"

"Well, I mean, not that good."

"Do you know what happened?"

Of course I know what happened. I burned down the Fort.

"I guess."

"Do you know what started the fire?"

I had never met Mr. Sanders in my life. I'm sure he had no idea who I was before this encounter. He was mostly bald with patches of white hair and a bushy mustache, also entirely white. Around school, he typically wore a sweater vest with an omnipresent school logo tie. He must have had a million sweater vests. On this night, however, he was wearing a full tuxedo with a red bow tie and matching cummerbund. This was the last thing he had expected from this supposedly festive evening. It was hardly the perfect setting for our introduction.

"I think it was a cigarette."

"A cigarette?" That would have been my father going off.

"You were smoking?" inquired the head.

It suddenly dawned on me, through the fog in my head, where this discussion was headed. I sat upright and looked about. There were hundreds of kids circled about and staring at me. Their dance obviously had experienced an abrupt ending, and I was now the best entertainment around. And while there were hundreds of kids, there was no Jelly and no Shaky. They were long gone.

No doubt they had already thought about this conversation I was about to have and what my answer might be.

"I guess," I lied.

"How did you get up there?"

"There's an entrance by the kitchen loading dock."

"That door has been locked for years."

"It was easy to break."

"And you were up there by yourself?"

I paused again.

"Yessir."

My father wasn't buying any of this, but he was the least of my problems at that moment. He wouldn't want me to get kicked out of school, so there was no way he was going to join in the inquisition.

"How often did you go up there?"

"Every once in a while."

"What did you do up there?"

"There were a lot of old newspapers. I would read them."

"You would read old newspapers?"

"Yessir." I felt better I didn't have to lie about that at least.

"How many old newspapers were there?"

"Pile after piles. Mostly old *Boston Globes* from the sixties and seventies. There were a few stacks of *The New York Times*, and every once in a while a *Wall Street Journal* would be stuck in between the stacks. But I didn't ever read those."

This was more than the headmaster wanted to hear. My mother was standing off by herself crying.

"Were you drinking?"

"Uh huh."

"By yourself?"

"Yes."

"What were you drinking?"

"Red wine."

"And where did you get the wine?"

This guy was no dummy. He'd done this many times before. I hesitated before my next lie.

"From my parents' house."

I didn't look up at my father. He knew it was a lie. My parents didn't drink. There was no alcohol in our house. But my father didn't say a word. I was trying my best to survive. And strangely enough he was helping me.

"You know that you are underage?"

"Yes."

"You know that drinking is against school rules?"

"Yes."

"And while we are thankful that you are alive, you may want to look up again at the Fort. You have managed by your actions to do what no one has ever done in the one hundred forty year history of this school, which is to burn down part of the Fort."

Ouch.

"You can go home now. We will talk tomorrow, Will. We will have a great deal to talk about, I suspect. In the meantime, I suggest you have your doctor check you out."

"Yessir."

My parents waited for me so that we could walk to the car together. I was shivering from the cold and the shame. I looked around at the many faces still standing and watching. No Jelly. No Shaky.

A sudden thought caused me to look back up at the Fort. Not the turret, but the last window on the third floor on the left. The light was on.

49.

"WILL, COME ON IN."

"Hi, Dr. Janos."

"You're early."

"It's a habit I've picked up. Kind of a rule around my house."

"You seem a little nervous."

"I've never been to see a psychologist before."

"Don't worry, that's what most of the kids say. I've seen two hundred sixty different kids so far this year from the school."

"Two hundred sixty?"

"Yup. It's not as unusual as you might think. Kids face a great deal of stress. Academic pressure. Social pressure. Parental pressure."

"That may be a little too easy for me."

"Yes. I understand you tried to burn down the Fort."

"Fortunately, I didn't completely succeed."

"But you're physically unharmed?"

"That is correct."

"Then why don't you sit down. Before they decide whether or not to expel you, they want me to assess whether you're a danger to the other students in the school."

"Huh?"

"A safety risk. Some of the parents are quite concerned. Many of them had children in the building—in the dorms or at the dance. If the fire had not been contained by the stone walls of the stairwell, their children might have been seriously hurt."

"I hadn't thought about that."

"That is called being a teenager. Teenagers often act impulsively without regard to the repercussions."

"That sounds like me."

I took a seat in front of the doctor's desk. It was no different from many of the other faculty offices. Small, spartan, with a few framed pictures of family on the desk. Nothing like what you see on television. I couldn't believe I was actually meeting with a psychologist. I certainly had my issues, but I didn't think that I was shrink-worthy by any means.

Dr. Janos looked like you would expect a psychologist to look. Smallish, a neatly trimmed beard, wire-rimmed glasses and a sweater with patches on the elbows. All he needed was the pipe and the Rorschach pictures.

"So tell me, why were you up in the Fort attic?"

"Mostly to get away."

"Get away from what?"

I really didn't know. The reality was that I was up there because my two friends dragged me up there. But since I was the only one who knew that, I couldn't say anything. As I was uncomfortable lying, I figured that I'd better try to change the direction of the conversation.

"Well, to lay it on the line, I'm just … growing up too fast. I don't want to."

"You don't want to grow up?"

"Not really."

"How come?"

"It doesn't look like any fun."

"Hmmm. That's a new twist. What do you like to do for fun, Will?"

"Play basketball. Chill, I guess."

"Do you like school?"

"Not really."

"Not really?"

"Well, I mean, I have some friends here and all. But I don't really understand its value. I don't have any interest in being a businessman or a lawyer or a doctor. I don't really care about money. I just want a simple life."

"There's certainly nothing wrong with that."

"Except that everyone here is such an overachiever."

"Don't be fooled by everything you read."

"Really?"

"Sure. There are a lot of very well off kids with highly motivated parents here. But it takes all types. Not all the kids are like their parents."

I actually was starting to like this guy, and I didn't mind the conversation. And it was a conversation rather than the inquisition I had been expecting.

"So where does that leave me?"

"What do you mean?"

"I have highly motivated parents who have given me what most would see as an incredible opportunity. We do fine, but aren't super rich. I think the tuition here is a big deal for them. Every time I seem to get myself focused in a good place, I seem to find a way to screw up. And this was a big screwup. How do I make it up to everybody for this?"

"Do you want to make it up?"

"Sure. I think so. I mean, I didn't want to hurt anyone in the Fort. I just don't always think ahead."

"That can usually be fixed if you want it be fixed."

"I think I do."

50.

THEY LET ME BACK into school after a two week suspension, but I was on an island. Radioactive. Everyone in the school now knew who I was, and some kids I had never spoken with before viewed me as a minor celebrity. But for the most part I stayed to myself, going to classes, doing homework, and going to bed. I was banned from regular after school activities and was to head straight home once the academic day was over. I also had to continue to see Dr. Janos every week. I don't think that he ever really found anything wrong with me, but it gave him something to do, and I continued to actually like the guy. He wasn't judgmental, which was a nice change for me. Mostly he just asked open-ended questions.

I still had not spoken with Jelly since the fire. Our eyes met a few times as we walked between classes, but she would quickly turn away. Shaky just never even looked. I wanted to believe they both felt guilty that I was receiving all the punishment for our collective actions, but I wasn't sure. It didn't really bother me, except that they weren't going to let me play basketball next year even though I had been elected one of the captains. They said that I was lucky to still be at the school and that captains could be replaced.

But the end of school came relatively painlessly. My father had set up a job for me in New York for the summer as an errand boy in a big law firm that did business with his company. He was calling in a favor. I wasn't particularly excited about the idea, but the reality was that I was in no position to bargain given my trespasses of the past month. Another part of my punishment was to write a hundred and fifty page thesis over the summer on someone that I found interesting. So I didn't expect I would have much free time anyway. Plus I was going to be living in a monastery in Connecticut, another connection my father had made. He figured if he had me live with a bunch of priests for a couple of months that their goodness might rub off on me.

The Saturday after the final day of classes, all of the underclassmen were required to don our costumes once again and attend the graduation ceremony for the seniors. The benefit of being a senior is that you didn't have to stay to take exams like the rest of us. I didn't mind being at graduation too much since it was better than studying, which was what I spent most of my time doing following my punishment.

The girls all wore white dresses and shoes. The boys were in their usual blue blazers but with white ties and white pants to match the girls' outfits. It presented a blaze of great whiteness, hope for their new futures.

As I sat near the back, I searched for Jelly out of habit. In fact, I almost missed her as she stood with another group of girls at the base of the portable stage, getting ready for the rite to begin. For the first time, she looked like the rest of them, wearing a white dress that came down to just above her knees, white stockings, and the same color shoes. No colored hair, only two earrings, no high tops, and for the first time I could remember in a long while she was wearing a bra.

It struck me how lonely I was. I watched her move lithely about the staging area with seemingly more grace than just a few months ago. She truly was beautiful when she dressed like a typical teenage girl. I guess that I had always found her tantalizing, even behind the colorful picture she painted. But in this new light she was even more of a treasure. I truly believed we had a special connection, even though I likely would never really be certain what our relationship was.

I turned to search the crowd. It didn't take long to figure out Laurel and Hardy given Hardy's large size and the fact they were holding hands. They sat side by side and were talking excitedly. The storm between them seemed to have subsided, so pleased to see their daughter in her moment of glory.

But for me I suspected the Jelly chapter was over.

51.

"Hey."

I twirled about, hearing the familiar greeting. Jelly, standing there in her glistening graduation dress, seemed so grown up and yet even more attractive than she'd been before. The ceremony was over, and I was walking by myself up the hill to the Fort to get some lunch.

"Hey."

She stared at her shoes for a moment while they played with some dirt below. I just looked at her like I used to.

"How are you?"

"Okay."

"Really?"

"I guess."

She seemed to be struggling with what to say, unusual for the girl who'd never been known to be shy.

So I helped her out.

"I haven't seen you for a while."

"Yeah, I know."

More silence.

"How come you didn't run?" I suspected she had been waiting for a while to ask me this. She probably had expected all of us to vanish and leave the Fort fire for the administration to figure out.

"I don't know. It didn't seem like the right thing to do."

"You got in a lot of trouble, didn't you?"

"You could say that."

"I'm sorry."

"They won't let me play basketball next year."

"I heard."

"And I have to write a hundred and fifty page thesis."

"I heard that too."

"I didn't think you cared."

"I care more than you know. I'll make it up to you."

"Don't worry about it. I'm tougher than I look."

"How are your parents taking it?"

"Better than I thought, actually. They didn't want to see me get expelled. And they know I wasn't alone."

"They do?"

"Yeah, they know I'd never smoke a cigarette. They've actually turned out to be okay through all this."

"Are you?"

"I hope so."

"Me too."

"Can I ask you a question?"

"Uh huh."

"How come *you* ran? I mean, I expected Shaky to run. It's part of his environment. People do stupid things, and they take off. But I didn't think that was in your genes."

"I panicked."

"You don't panic. You're the coolest person I've ever seen under pressure. You buck the dress code. You invite me up to your room to get naked in the middle of the day. You …"

"I thought Princeton would yank my college acceptance."

That was not the answer that I had expected from Jelly. In fact, it was probably the last answer that I expected to hear coming from her lips. It made me angry. For the first time I considered that maybe she was just like all the other kids after all.

"I didn't think it was that important to you."

"I quickly realized it was."

"Very quickly."

"Yeah."

"You surprised me, that's all."

"I feel like a shit. I'll make it up to you."

"Don't make promises you can't keep."

"I will make it up to you."

"Jelly, you're going to college! I'll be stuck here on my island, writing my thesis and going nowhere fast. We're going two different ways now."

"Maybe we can do stuff this summer."

"I'll be working in Manhattan."

"Really?"

"Yeah."

"Does this mean you don't love me anymore?"

"Jelly, I can finally admit that I'll probably never stop loving you. I just don't know if I can forgive you."

"I promise I'll make it up to you."

"I already told you. Don't make promises you can't keep."

52.

Mr. Bussmann died of a heart attack the following Monday. Apparently his weight and his smoking caught up with him. He collapsed in the middle of his freshman math final exam, and neither the school nurse nor the paramedics could revive him. A whole class of kids watched the dean of discipline die.

My grandfather was the only person I'd known who had died, and he lived pretty far away, so I rarely saw him. All of the rest of my grandparents, aunts and uncles were alive. Same for neighbors and friends. There had been a kid on my street who was really sick with a rare form of cancer when he was four and almost died. But the treatment worked, and he was fine and going to college some place in Colorado.

But I'd known Mr. Bussmann. He'd been my teacher my first year. We'd had a somewhat turbulent relationship between the cheating accusation, punching incident, and his making me do the play. But still I'd had many interactions with him over the last three years—some quite serious and some matter of fact. Sometimes I thought he really cared for me as a student. Other times I could never tell if he ever had fully forgiven me for punching him.

Now he was dead. The whole school came to a sort of standstill. After all, he had been there a long time and was a pretty visible figure. I was sure his poor personal habits would remain a lesson to all of us students for many years to come. But maybe not. I think that, on the whole, people in my circle had pretty short memories.

For much of the first several days after he died I tried to figure out how I felt about his passing. I wasn't really sure. They had a school-wide service for him. And Dr. Janos was out in full force offering his counsel to any student or faculty member who wanted to talk. I figured Dr. Janos had already seen enough of me. Plus I wasn't confused. Death was a part of life. It happened to everyone. When it was time, it was time.

Shaky had once said that after he saw his parents murdered it would be hard for him to feel any sadness when someone else died—except for maybe his grandmother. He had made the decision not to get too close to anyone so he wouldn't ever be hurt again.

I could understand Shaky's perspective. Death was far less uncommon in his world than in mine. Maybe it was just that for the first time I was facing a world of mortality. And while he wasn't family or a close friend, Mr. Bussmann was someone who I had come to share a space with over the last three years. Only I would be here tomorrow and he wouldn't.

53.

FOUR BOYS FROM ANOTHER private school in our area were expelled during the winter for having a fifteen year old girl perform oral sex on them in the locker room. They were all football players. One of them was celebrating a birthday. The incident has been turned over to the police. Some of the boys were old enough to be tried as adults. And because of the girl's age the charge could be statutory rape. It has been front page news on and off for the past semester.

Part of me was grateful I'd never had to deal with this type of activity with Will. I suspect there had been temptations with Jelly, but I think his values are okay on the whole. The other part of me asked what the hell was I doing introducing him to this kind of spoiled, rich kid, prep school environment. These kids were so entitled that they could force little girls to give half the team oral sex?

I was still stuck with my conviction that Will wasn't a bad kid. Just a little confused. I just hoped that I was right. He was lucky the fire in the Fort hadn't hurt anybody. Buildings can be repaired. But I knew he hadn't been up there alone. Will would never smoke. Sports were too important to him. And Amy and I don't drink. So there wasn't any wine in our home. Whoever had been up there with him had brought the wine and the cigarettes and had gotten a free ride. It didn't make what Will did any more right. But some kids' records were going be unblemished when they shouldn't have been. It wasn't fair.

Even before the Fort fire I'd been spending more and more nights lying awake in bed wondering whether this was all worth it. We still had two more kids behind Will to raise, and we were quickly getting burned out. I felt like I never had a break from the anxiety that Will's indifference was causing inside of me.

Maybe it was time to lay off. Amy had more and more been openly pushing for that as the year progressed. Let him figure it out for himself. Let him sink or swim on his own. She was probably right, but the more I worried, the less I seemed inclined to let him go. So instead I pulled in a few favors and got Will a job in New York and a place to live with a bunch of priests. I was hopeful they wouldn't find him fodder for their own fun as too many priests had been doing in Boston. I was more hopeful that a fresh new set of voices would help him find himself and his values. My message certainly hadn't gotten through yet, so I thought maybe theirs would.

54.

DARIEN WAS PART OF what they called the Connecticut Gold Coast. I was to live there for the summer in a small, spartan room with a crucifix that hung vacantly on the wall above my laptop and a nondescript Catholic-issue desk. Each morning, from Monday to Friday, my role was to walk from the rectory to the Darien train station to make the trek into New York City to my summer job as a gofer in a law firm. The train station was essentially a huge parking lot full of Land Rovers, Lexuses, and Suburbans that surrounded a tiny, little, brown shingled building where coffee and newspapers were sold. A couple of Hummers waited each day for those at the head of the pack; a sprinkling of Jeep Cherokees for the ones not yet there. Custom tailored suits, understated but expensive jewelry, every top ten selling electronic gadget. Except for the tailored suits, this parking lot was much like the student lot at Pendy.

I suspected that for most of the people who rode this train day in and day out it was a mainly forgettable part of their lives. Faceless, nameless men and women in navy blue and charcoal gray, in solids and pinstripes, who turned off their persona for the fifty-five minute ride from my summer town or the sixty-three minute commute back and forth to Rowayton. Two hours a day on the train. Five days a week, fifty-two weeks a year save holidays and vacations. Some read or pretended to read the *Wall Street Journal* or *The New*

York Times. Many preferred to be reading the *Daily News* but were too embarrassed to be seen by potential friends or possible clients. Sometimes they napped; some just gazed out the window as the suburban blandness gave way to the demoralizing blight of the Bronx and then, ultimately, the electricity of Manhattan. It was great people watching.

Even during my short summer in New York, I read more newspaper stories than I can ever remember, took my share of naps, and memorized every house, building, and unintelligible scribbling of graffiti along the thirty-eight miles of tracks between my platform and Grand Central Station. Apparently almost four hundred thousand passengers rode this line each year. For most, the second week of June turned into the third week of July, which turned into the fourth week of August. And if I were to lie down in bed one night and never wake up, none of them would have ever noticed me missing.

In truth, the Connecticut Gold Coast should have been annexed by New York long ago. The television channels, radio stations and newspapers were all New York. The employment base was Manhattan. The Connecticut address somehow managed to keep taxes lower and real estate prices higher. The prospect of living in the metropolis would have been scary for a young man of nondescript roots and no backbone like me. Visiting was okay since I could still hop the train out before Gotham overwhelmed.

The rattle and rock of the tired train quickly became inharmoniously familiar. The sounds of the doors opening and closing between cars, the conductor's hole puncher validating tickets in the antiquated, union protected ticketing system, the squeals as the rusty metal wheels slowly made the turns along the rail. I got the sense that not much managed by the transit authority ever changed.

"Is this seat taken?"

"No. Better grab it while you can."

I removed the pages clutching the *Daily News* sports section that I had just finished and had set aside on the orange plastic seat to my side.

"You know, you look a bit young to be in the bar car."

"It was the only open seat I could find."

"How old are you? Twenty?"

"Seventeen."

"I promise I won't tell."

The soft British accent of the man in the expensive blue double-breasted pinstriped suit with his tie still knotted to the top of his shirt was equally as ill-fitting as I was in the bar car, where patrons were packed elbow to elbow like cattle about to be branded, drowning the day's stock market losses in hard drink and cursing the slump of their Yankees.

I had actually lied to him. I had been sitting in the bar car for the entire first two weeks of my summer, being a total wallflower and never drinking but enjoying much more the people watching in this section than the others. The liquor must have been reasonably toxic; I would watch people quickly lose all inhibitions after they grabbed their first drink. Vodka martinis in opaque plastic cups seemed to be the common denominator. I often wished I had my camera with me.

"They make these drinks incredibly strong," the Brit offered. He had a drink in each hand. "Most nights by the time the train pulls up to my platform, I've got quite a good buzz going."

"I wouldn't really know."

"Don't touch the stuff?"

"Not old enough."

"Yes. I guess that's right. Good for you. Back home in London we start much too young."

"Your wife and kids must love that."

"Hardly. No wife, no kids. But you've made me feel sufficiently guilty. Here, take one of my drinks."

I did as I was told.

"Aren't you kind of old not to be married?"

"There are many others who have hinted at the same. Never been married. I go home to an empty house. So if I fall asleep after too much liquor, no one cares."

"Don't worry. My life isn't too exciting either. I'm living in a rectory for the summer. I get home and have supper with a bunch of priests."

The Brit I would later come to know as Gerald. For as long as I knew him that summer, he would be tastefully appointed, from the always trimmed black hair to the mirror-like shine on his shoes. The slight paunch of his mid-section was perpetually hidden by his buttoned suit coat. Pasty white skin was interrupted only by two rosy pink cheeks. He had been here for almost twenty years. A transplant from Great Britain, the bar car had become his motor home.

"That must be rather uninteresting."

"It keeps me out of trouble. But it sounds like your social life is no better."

It was easy to talk to a man that I was initially fairly certain I would never see again. I suspected that he felt the same way.

"I actually have no desire to marry. But to avoid any unfounded rumors, rest assured that does not squelch my intent to be with women as often as I possibly can."

"Oh. Is it reciprocal?"

The first vodka martini was apparently quite strong. Plus I still couldn't hold my liquor. A keen delight was already beginning to run laps inside my head. Nonetheless, Gerald appeared to find the discussion sufficiently entertaining.

"Forgive my lack of modesty, my man, but I've had plenty of women since I've been here. I like it over here in States. Many women find me attractive."

"Really? How many?"

"More than I can remember. They are, on the whole, quite accommodating."

"Accommodating? I mean, I don't get it. You certainly dress well. But you're chubby, pasty faced, and it seems to me that you walk with a waddle. No offense intended."

It was the booze talking. I would never otherwise have been that bold with a grown man.

"None taken. It's the accent. Works every time."

"You mean if I talked with your ridiculous accent, women would start walking up and asking me to have their babies?"

I may have been beginning to slur my words. True to form, it didn't take much to get me drunk. I'd actually never had hard liquor before.

"If you looked older than fourteen, I imagine some women might."

"Puberty has been slow in coming."

I remember chuckling to myself at the thought. I expected it would be a long time coming before I was deemed attractive by older women. Hell, I still didn't even really shave.

"Why do you live in the suburbs rather than Manhattan?" I asked.

"You're kidding, aren't you? That place gets scary when the sunlight goes down. Besides, they have more money out here. And bigger breasts, even if some of them aren't real."

He was so different from my father, though not much younger I suspected.

"How often do you go out?"

"I could go out on a different date every night if I desired."

"Aren't you a bit overconfident?"

"Just reviewing the facts, my friend."

"Do you have sex with them?"

I couldn't believe I'd asked him that. The words just came pouring out on their own.

"Sometimes. Problem is that too often after I have had a few too many drinks, young Thaddeus doesn't stand at attention."

"Thaddeus?"

"Yes. What do you call yours?"

"My what?"

"Your Thaddeus."

"Johnson, usually."

I had no idea. I just made that up. Maybe I'd heard it before.

"Thaddeus reflects a greater pedigree."

"Woody." To our surprise, a middle-aged commuter, barrel chested and athletic looking with much gray growing around the ears, had been eavesdropping. "Sorry, I couldn't help myself. Hope you don't mind, but you have to admit it's been a rather unusual dialogue. You're also probably corrupting the kid."

"Yes, I guess indeed I am. But then again someone has to," opined Gerald. "Now I don't mind the eavesdropping a bit, but the next round of liquor will have to be on you."

"I can agree to that."

A middle-aged woman with frosted hair and big, formerly firm breasts ducked her head into our now circle of four.

"If I join this conversation, does that mean I have to buy a round as well?"

"Absolutely," Gerald grinned. "It's our rule."

It had been a long time since I had been at the center of such animated and growing dialogue. Usually I wasn't very good at group talk. This was all very new to me. I had finished my first drink but had no intention of giving up my spot in this expanding entourage. The train ride home took an hour, so there was still more entertainment to come. This slightly pudgy Brit was bold, disarmingly straightforward, and charming, and he certainly was quickly attracting a crowd—which was more than I could ever claim. I really had a major buzz going.

"So you guys name your things?" the women asked with great curiosity and a snicker.

"Yes, but it is not a simple process. Which of our names would you choose?"

"What are the choices again?"

"Johnson, Woody, and Thaddeus." He even chuckled with a British accent.

"Thaddeus, of course."

"Why?" argued the other man.

"The greater pedigree, of course."

We all had a good laugh, save the other man who, it was clear, was already too drunk to appreciate the unusual humor in our conversation. It was not a story he would want to bring home and tell the family anyway. She, on the other hand, was an interesting woman. Makeup, manicure, curls, lots of expensive looking jewelry but no wedding ring. You quickly got the sense that she would be quite comfortable telling crude jokes and smoking cigars with the guys.

"But you can't go out with a new woman every night!" I pleaded, wanting in earnest for the dialogue to return to its original roots. I couldn't believe they were even letting me stay in the conversation.

"Sure I can."

"I'm willing to put my money against that. Here's twenty bucks," muddled the other man.

"I'm in," said the woman.

"You don't take long to join in the party, do you?" Gerald looked at his new doubter.

I didn't say anything because I didn't have twenty dollars to spare.

"Here, cutey." The unknown woman turned to me. "You hold the money."

Without speaking further to us, Gerald approached a tall, red haired woman not more than five feet away from my new circle of acquaintances. Tall and trim, she was probably six or eight years younger than he was. He showed not the slightest trace of nerves. The rest of us watched in fascination.

"Excuse me. I don't do this often, but I saw you and thought you were fascinating." The British accent was more pronounced than it had been during our train gang's conversation. "Is there any chance you might like to have dinner with me?"

She didn't appear to be bothered by the attention.

"I detect an accent. Are you new to this country?"

"No, actually I've been here for near twenty years."

"How do I know you aren't a mad stalker?"

"Oh, well I actually am." He pulled out his business card and handed it to her. "They couldn't quite fit it on the card."

She first eyed the card and flipped it in her hand; then she turned her gaze at him. Incredibly, she had already been taken with his approach and the shit-eating grin on his face.

"And exactly how often do you ask a random woman on the train for a date after telling her she is 'fascinating'?"

"It probably occurs more frequently than I should admit. The alcohol takes away some of the fear."

"How do you know I'm not married?"

"I haven't seen a ring."

"How do you know I'm not dating someone?"

"You don't seem to be in a rush to get home. You're in the bar car. If you were getting ready to see a mate, you would more likely be in one of the normal cars preening. But then again, I am only guessing."

"Unfortunately you guessed right."

"Does that mean we have a date?"

This woman looked him over from head to toe. He grinned the whole time, not quite yet a drunk's grin.

"My name is Charlotte."

"Well, Charlotte, what say I pick you up tomorrow at seven o'clock?"

She took his card and wrote down her address and phone number. She was clearly amused and pleased. Gerald, in time, turned back to his new friends.

"This should help pay for a nice dinner." He took the two twenty dollar bills that I had been holding, folded them together and tucked the money into his breast pocket.

"Unbelievable," our drunk new friend slurred.

"I am impressed," expressed the big breasted woman.

The train curdled and screeched while the conductor made a muffled announcement of another stop.

"Well, here's where I get out."

"Are we ever going to hear the aftermath of your date? We want to make sure she isn't your sister or college roommate."

"Fair enough. For those of you who can remember, we shall meet here same time, same place on Friday. Got it, Ace?" Gerald chuckled at the drunk who was far enough gone that he would surely miss his stop.

"Huh?"

So this was how grownups who weren't my parents really acted when they weren't on stage.

55.

THE NEXT DAY I thought a lot about that train ride home. It was as close to an out-of-body experience as I'd ever had. I'd never, ever been so brazen with anyone, particularly an adult who I had never previously met. But truth be told I kind of liked it. It was like living in a world of make believe. I could be whoever I wanted, and there were no consequences to anything I'd say. Maybe the summer wouldn't be as bad as I had anticipated.

So Friday came, and I hustled my way to Grand Central Station, making sure I was positioned by the track properly to get to the bar car quickly. I had been looking forward to this trip all day. I didn't know whether Gerald, the celebrity of our first meeting, or the others would show. But I was not going to miss it if they did.

The train out of Grand Central is long, but the bar car, being at the back of the train, is closest to the station's staging area; hence the closest doorway to the bar car is typically mobbed. I almost threw aside other commuters as I thrust my way through the train door, like a salmon battling upstream to spawn eggs, or in this case to hear the tale of my new mentor.

As I slid open the final compartment doors to the bar car, I was stunned to find Ace and the woman whose name I did not yet know already there waiting patiently for Gerald. They noticed me immediately.

"No offense," offered Ace, "but we were hoping you were the British fellow."

"How long have you been here?"

"What do you think?" he asked the woman. "Perhaps ten minutes?"

She nodded. Each had a plastic cup already half emptied of a drink. Their Friday evenings had started a little before mine.

I had to admit being surprised. Given Ace's condition the other night, I didn't think that he would have ever remembered our planned rendezvous. Ace gulped the remainder of his drink and turned to head toward the union bar.

"By the way," he asked before setting out, "did you notice anyone else in our company here tonight?"

I looked about but could not identify any familiar face.

"To the rear of the car, with a group of horny younger men. Recognize the woman?"

I squinted and vaguely remembered.

"Was that our objective from the other night?" the woman asked.

"It was indeed."

"Well, at least our man didn't turn out to be a mass killer."

I watched Ace as he parted the waves on his way to the bar. Ace would turn out to be an interesting fellow. Sober, he was personable and engaging, a fit and handsome man. Probably six foot two, he carried himself with the swagger of a former athlete, and his attire certainly placed him in the upper echelon of business commuters. A stark contrast to me in my well-worn school blazer and khakis. He seemed, however, to have a more than capable appetite for alcohol, and the person he became after a few drinks was nothing like the original. As I was learning, alcohol could do strange things to you.

"You know, I probably should introduce myself since we are here as a group tonight. I am Catherine, but please call me Cat. I don't like 'Catherine.'"

"That's my grandmother's name."

"Do you like your grandmother?"

"A lot. She's the only laid back one in my family."

"So what's your name?"

"I'm Will."

"Well, Will, not to cut short our formal introduction, but look who just walked in."

Entering through the same compartment door was our Brit, suitably attired in another double-breasted suit that hugged his modest paunch and not a bit of a change in his pasty white skin and rosy cheeks. He nodded to us at once.

"Well, did you come to place another wager?"

The group had naturally saved a seat for Gerald. It was the same plastic booth we had shared two evenings before.

"So how did it go, your honor? Did you enjoy your date?" asked Cat. She hadn't taken her eyes off him since he had stuck his head into the bar car.

"Yes, in fact. It was quite nice. And feel free to call me Gerald. Many people do."

"She actually showed up for your date?"

"Yes, in fact I think she bought a new outfit and everything. She was quite smashing."

"Did Thaddeus get to enjoy himself?" Ace was back with drinks.

"My, aren't we inquisitive." Gerald for the first time looked at Cat, their eyes locking briefly. "I think we'll save that discussion for another time." He turned to our fourth partner, who quickly was on his way once again. "Well, Ace," he said with more than a little condescension, "how are we today?"

"Not as well as you. You got it last night, and I haven't gotten it in seventeen months. But who the hell's counting?"

So that accounts for the heavy drinking.

Gerald jumped in.

"Okay, hold on a minute here. We all seem to be enjoying pontificating about my sex life, and I don't even know who you people are yet. So what say we cover the basics first, and then we'll get back to the sex?"

"Works for me," I tossed in.

"Okay, you start," commanded Cat.

"Fair enough, but Ace, you owe us a round of drinks. I think it's about time to get after it."

Ace grumbled something or other but stood and began to bull his way once more across the familiar path to the bar.

"Excuse me, is anybody sitting here?"

Once more each of us looked up, this time to see a younger woman with a boyish haircut, probably in her early thirties, dressed in a green army uniform. She was looking to secure Ace's seat.

"Do we have to salute?" chimed Cat.

"Not if you don't want to," the young woman responded.

"Well, I'm going to salute," claimed Gerald, raising his hand to his forehead. "That way I won't feel bad when we start asking her all of her own darkest secrets."

The woman giggled nervously, obviously having no idea what the hell we were talking about. Her smile was great. A big set of white teeth and big dimples the size of half moons. She gratefully seated herself in Ace's spot, and the discussion swung back to Gerald.

"So what do you do for a living?" I asked Gerald innocently.

"I'm a banker."

"Like one of those flashy investment bankers trying to do overpriced acquisitions or take crappy little companies public and fleece the little investor?" asked Cat.

"No. The kind that makes loans to companies—or I should say *tries* to make loans to companies. We're so damn slow, and we draw the process out so long that by the time we're ready to move the borrower usually no longer needs our money."

"So are you a banking star?" Ace was back, in gear with a handful of drinks, including one he handed to me without thinking, not wanting to miss the juicier conversation.

"Hardly."

"You certainly dress the part."

"Unfortunately that's probably my best skill. By the way, how do you get drinks so quickly?"

"They know I tip really well. Man, it didn't take you long to give away my seat."

"She's better looking than you are, Ace. You'll have to stand for now. No room at the inn."

Gerald sipped at the contents of his plastic cup as he talked. He had a habit of holding an ice cube in his mouth to chew on while working on his drink. Conversely, Ace would constantly stir his drink clockwise with his forefinger.

"So you aren't a banking star?"

"I've never made a loan in my career. In fact, I barely understand all the financial stuff I'm supposed to look at. I'm actually terrible at what I do."

"Then how do you keep your job?"

"Well, I do work hard at looking like I know what I'm doing. I get to my desk early and read the *Wall Street Journal* cover to cover. Don't understand most of it. Spend the whole day on the phone—at least that's what the bank thinks I do. Sometimes I'm just talking to the fellow who sits in front of me. Sometimes there is no one on the other end of the phone, and I just pretend to talk. But I suspect that the greatest reason I'm there is that my boss is a thirty-nine year old single bitch who hears the ticking clock and can't find a husband. I figure she is keeping me around as a last resort."

"So what about you? How come they call you Ace?"

"They don't."

"What do you mean?

"You guys are the only ones who call me Ace."

"I thought that was your name."

"My name is Walter."

"I don't much like that name."

"That must be why you've taken to calling me Ace."

"You don't mind, do you?"

"No, not really."

Walter, or Ace as we started calling him, had probably been a stud in his younger days. He still had all his hair, though he was obviously crossing the fifty-yard line in age.

"So what do you do, Ace?"

"I work for my wife's company. Have ever since we married. Her old man died a decade ago, so I now run the show."

"What is the company?"

"We sell ladies' underwear."

Gerald's drink almost came out of his nose.

"That's not a business. That's an act you can get arrested for!"

"Don't I know it."

"Does your wife work there too?"

"Only when she wants to try to give me a coronary."

"Things aren't sunny on the home front?

"I don't think my wife finds me appealing anymore," Ace mumbled. "I think she's been contemplating having an affair. She's stopped wearing her wedding ring most of the time."

"Well, why don't we find out?"

"What do you mean?"

"I'll ask her out."

"What makes you think she'll go with you?"

"Haven't we already established that?"

"Are you planning to bring Thaddeus?" Cat chimed in.

"You guys are sick."

"Okay, new girl, tell the truth."

"My name's Libby."

"Okay, Libby, would you rather go out with a Woody, a Johnson, or a Thaddeus?"

"Boy, we didn't waste any time bringing her down to our depraved level."

"Don't worry," countered our newest friend with a soft laugh. "I'm in the army, remember?"

"So, Libby, what do you do for the army?" Gerald was going to let her off the hook.

"I'm a recruiter."

"How long have you been in the army?"

"Fourteen years. Since high school."

"So, Miss Army Recruiter, did you recruit anybody today?"

"Four unemployed, bigoted assholes and one hot, blonde coed."

"Excuse me?"

"Are you interested?"

"I'm not sure."

"Oh, from the other team, huh?" Ace had a way with words.

"Wait. Libby can't have an opinion then," argued Cat with no one in particular.

"An opinion on what?"

"Our existential debate. Thaddeus, Johnson, or Woody. Where have you been?"

"Right here, I thought." Ace was fading fast. "Why can't she offer her opinion?"

"She's from the other team, Ace. She doesn't want to go out with any of them."

Incredible. These were my new teachers. My summer school faculty.

56.

At the start of the summer I never paid much attention to which train I caught to come home. If they still had gofer work for me to do at the office I would stay and finish it up. There was never much occasion to hustle to catch a train since I never really had anything to get home to do except to work on my thesis. The priests didn't even have a television. But my urgency had changed.

My life for these few short summer weeks strangely centered around that train ride home. I barely knew their names, knew little of their backgrounds, had never seen them anywhere outside of the silver mule. But since I could essentially be anyone I wanted to be, I knew there was no way in hell I was going to miss one of our train gang's highly unpredictable rides to the suburbs. Without any formal planning, we had evolved into a regular pattern. I'd arrive at the station first, board the train, hustle to the bar car and reserve our regular spot. Gerald, Cat, and Ace would wait for each other in the station lobby until the final announcement and then board the train ensemble. Ace, followed by Gerald, would make the run to the bar and bring back the same drinks for each, including me. They would all throw a few dollars on the table that Gerald would collect, neatly organize and divide between himself and Ace. While Libby was still a bit of an outsider, she would increasingly join us for our postwork rendezvous.

"So who shall we make miserable today?" asked Cat as we all sat down in our usual spot. The union had run out of ice that day, so our plastic cup drinks were warm—feeling not unlike when you pee in a cup at the doctor's office.

"I think that we've let Will off the hook long enough," suggested Gerald.

This was just so different from school. Since I would never see these people again after the summer had ended, I was not at all concerned with what might be asked or what I might respond. Plus the liquor took the edge off everything.

"So, Will, you're a bad ass college freshman, huh?"

"Just finished my junior year in high school."

"You're not old enough to drink, are you?" guessed the army woman.

"No."

"Don't worry. It's good for you. It'll put hair on your chest."

"And you live in Darien by yourself?"

"Just for the summer. In a rectory with priests."

This time Ace nearly snarfed his drink out of his nose.

"They all want to be your roommate?"

"No."

"Are you sure?"

"Not really."

"Bingo."

"Are you gay?" asked Cat.

It was Gerald who snarfed his drink following that comment.

"My God, woman. Have you no decency?"

"No, I'm not gay. At least I don't think so. But I've been out on dates with a girl only twice, and it really didn't work out too well either time."

"How come?"

"Well, on our first date I learned she was a lesbian. On our second I burned down a building by mistake."

"Ouch."

"Did they kick you out?

"No. I just have to write a long thesis."

"About what?"

"I'm haven't really figured that out yet. I'm supposed to write about someone I find interesting, but I haven't found anyone I am interested in enough to write a hundred and fifty pages about."

"Then how about your experiences this summer with us?" Cat joked. "I am certain we could be entertaining for a whole variety of reasons."

"I expect it would be a bestseller," Gerald smiled.

They all laughed.

"And you haven't gotten back on the horse, Will?"

"Too much effort."

"I think you must be gay," chimed in Libby.

"Words from our resident expert."

"I think you're wrong."

"I don't think I am."

"How do you really know?"

"Shall I prove it to you?"

"How?"

"There's a restroom here on the bar car." I don't think I really meant what I said. It was certainly the booze talking once again, not me.

Libby curled up her nose.

"Restrooms are gross."

"Way too grubby."

"I've used this one. It's brand new." I didn't know Ace was even listening.

"We are talking about a public bathroom, aren't we?"

Libby looked over at me. She knew that I was just a kid, but I think she was thinking more about herself. For a moment I thought of Jelly. A professed lesbian who couldn't help but to test herself with me. Maybe Libby shared that same uncertainty. Maybe I just had a special scent that attracted lesbians.

She grabbed my hand.

"Okay, let's give it a go."

With that the young army sergeant led me to the latrine. The other three sets of eyes, I have no doubt, followed in astonishment.

"Do they think they'll cure each other?" I heard Ace ask.

"To each his own, Ace. By the way, when are we going to cure your situation?"

"You mean my wife?"

Could you imagine if my father was witnessing this? I'd be grounded for life.

57.

LIBBY AND I HADN'T spoken a word. At first I didn't know if she or I was going to go through with it. So I let her take the lead, particularly since I really didn't know what I was doing. We brazenly entered the cramped bar car bathroom together, and after we kissed a little she changed her mind. I'd like to think that it wasn't me who turned her off but rather that she recognized she wasn't attracted to men—or perhaps that she was thirty-two and I was seventeen and having intercourse with me would be a crime. Or perhaps the public bathroom on the train was too much of a turn off. So the initial thrill subsided, but it was a thrill for a few minutes nonetheless.

At some point we returned to our group. I think we had only been gone about twenty minutes or so. The train was pulling into Darien, where Ace, Gerald, and I would disembark. Ace, while still his usual, manly self, had the mean drunk grimace on his face once again. My well-oiled friends were still in the middle of the same conversation they had been having when we had left on our little research project.

I could see Ace waving his hand at the Brit.

"Feel free to have at her. She's a tough bitch. You can't have any less luck with her than I do."

"Are you sure you want me to do this?"

"She'll be at the station tonight picking me up. I'll introduce you."

"How will you do that?"

Even Cat recognized the incredulity of the conversation. Her eyes met Gerald's, but he simply smiled and looked back at Ace.

"She'll be the one I kiss on the cheek, like Judas."

"So is our man gay?"

"Nope." She sounded confident in her answer.

"How about you? Does that mean you're not gay?'

"I think the answer is I am."

My sense was that I was getting good looking. I mean I was pretty happy with what I saw when I looked in the mirror. And my height helped. But I really had to start figuring out if I could attract straight women.

58.

"Excuse me, but I believe your husband may have fallen asleep on the train and missed his stop."

The British accent was in full bloom. The woman looked toward the departing train.

"It wouldn't be the first time," the woman said, as indignant at Ace as she could be.

I watched from a short distance. Most of the other commuters quickly scattered, as was their habit, to their cars in the parking lot. Ace's wife and Gerald remained stuck in conversation on the platform, like in a made-for-television movie. Even for a middle-aged woman she was really good looking.

"I'm sorry."

"It's not your fault."

"I've chatted with him a bit over the past few weeks. Seems to be a nice fellow."

"He's a shit."

Gerald paused momentarily.

"Since you don't have anything to do, can I take you to dinner?"

"Are you married?" she responded incredibly.

"No."

"You're not?"

"No, but you are."

"Yes. I thought you were, too."

"How come?"

"I didn't think any attractive single men lived in the suburbs."

Gerald knew I was there on the train platform, just a few feet away, but he had no problem performing for an audience.

"Sorry to disappoint you, but I've never been married. In fact, I've never even been close. But I am delighted to hear that someone finds me attractive."

"Well, I have to admit to being surprised."

"Do you do this often?"

"Do what?"

"Cheat on your husband."

"First time."

"I noticed you remembered to remove your wedding ring."

"Aren't I supposed to in these situations?"

"To tell you the truth I wouldn't know. But it does seem as if you have been planning ahead."

"Why don't you get your car and follow me. I know a quiet little tavern we can visit."

Incredible.

59.

THERE WAS A CERTAIN intrigue to this group of people. My new role models. They each were living lives more adventuresome, more glamorous than my simple existence. But in a few brief weeks I'd almost had sex for the first time in my seventeen years, and I'd watched an extramarital affair begin right under my nose and with the knowledge of the wronged spouse to boot. And we were going to hear Gerald's recap. In my simple life it didn't get any better than this.

Ace was visibly nervous; it was showtime for him. His intimate life, a thirty year marriage to a stunningly attractive woman and two resulting teenage children (my peers, interestingly enough), was going to be fodder for the whole gang. Because none of us ever saw each other outside of our commute, we had not yet shown any signs of being guarded with our comments. Even my eternally shy and boring character was continuing, on occasion, to show signs of emotional life that hadn't heretofore been witnessed.

"Ace, she thinks you're boring."

Ace looked up from his orange seat, his suit jacket off and folded on his lap, the knot in his tie loosened. Gerald had been a few steps behind him in the pilgrimage from the bar but had wasted no time in launching into his commentary. We had only fifty-five minutes to Darien, and that evening's topic promised to be fertile.

"That's what I was afraid of." He slumped in his chair.

"Okay, let's hear it," demanded Libby. "You guys have stuck your noses into my screwed up life sufficiently. It's time to change the target."

"What do you say, Ace? Want the details?"

I suspected Gerald was going to provide full disclosure whether Ace protested or not. He was just pretending to be polite.

"I doubt that I do."

"Well, I'm going to give them to you anyway." Bingo.

Ace took another long drag on his drink. Not a hair out of place, not a wrinkle in expensive his shirt, and dejected as hell.

"She and I went to a nice little restaurant in Rowayton. She didn't wear her ring, figuring that this was the appropriate thing to do. Don't worry, Ace. She is new at this."

"Did you sleep with her?"

"Why does everyone find my sex life so appealing?" Gerald shrieked. "Of course I didn't sleep with her. She's your wife, and you're my new friend. I wouldn't do that to you."

"So you're not going out again?"

"I didn't say that. We're going out tomorrow night. She's absolutely delightful. Besides, I need to help you out."

"You're going out with Ace's wife again?" Libby laughed in disbelief.

"Will you all just shut up for once so I can fill you in? If we're going to be commuting amigos, you will have to learn to be more considerate listeners."

None of the group even dared to make a noise. Gerald had us all so captivated with various levels of astonishment.

"I guess you two started dating in college."

"She was a couple of years younger than me."

"Yes, so she mentioned. She said you were the big man on campus. Smart, athletic, sexy. Tailor-made for Hollywood."

"Damn right."

"Were you rich when she married you?"

"I was smart, good looking, and great in the sack."

"So I've heard."

"And I was poor as dirt. I don't ever want to go back there again."

"So what the hell happened? She said the two of you used to be rabbits."

"Oh now we're talking about *my* sex life?"

"C'mon, Ace. Get with the program. Mine is regular fodder. Will and Libby screwed in the bathroom. We'll solve your problems; then we'll attack Cat's."

I sheepishly looked at Libby, and we blushed in concert.

"I'll warn you in advance," pronounced Cat. "Mine will be a short, uneventful discussion."

Gerald glanced at her quickly, and their eyes met. Clearly she too was falling fast into the Brit's trance.

"Anyway, Ace. She says you've gotten lazy. You drink too much, and as we can all see, you're getting fat. And from what I can understand you do a crappy job running her father's company. Hell, Ace, how the hell hard can selling ladies' underwear be?"

"You'd be surprised."

"Look, I may be a lousy banker, but women's underwear? You just keep reducing the amount of fabric and jacking up the price."

"But what about when your wife questions every decision you make, overturns your decisions with the staff, cancels you company credit card, and doesn't even wear the underwear you sell because it reminds her of you?"

A pause settled over the whole group.

"Now that's a problem," Gerald and Cat responded almost simultaneously.

Where was my camera?

60.

GERALD, CAT, AND I had already commenced our usual routine in the bar car. Libby was late—and breathless when she finally arrived. She was even more animated than usual, particularly for a Monday train ride. There was a glow in her face, and this from the most shy of our group.

"They were closing the doors. I had to talk them into letting me on."

"Is our timid friend becoming aggressive?"

"I told them I was pregnant and had to get to a doctor's appointment."

"Is it Will's baby?"

Libby didn't bother to answer. She was wearing the biggest grin I had ever seen her wear.

"What got you so excited today, little girl?"

Cat could on occasion demean Libby. Probably she was jealous of Libby's youth and still hard body. Plus, although Libby had announced her sexual preference, I still suspected that both Gerald and Ace would have welcomed the opportunity, if it arose, to try to make a woman out of her. I had obviously been given the chance but had failed miserably. But I could always use the excuse that I was new at this.

"Remember the girl I told you about at the recruiting office a few weeks ago?"

"Of course," said Gerald, our group ready to engage in another hour of sociology class.

"Well, we went out this weekend."

"What exactly does that mean?"

"We went on a date."

"How did you determine she was gay?"

"She's not sure, but she was willing to at least experiment a little."

"You like her?"

"Very much."

"Did you have sex?"

"Here we go again," I offered.

"Just a little."

"How can you have just a little sex?"

"We just kissed a little."

"Was she as good as Will?"

"Does kissing actually count as sex?"

"Just a little sex."

Libby looked at me again, this time smiling rather than blushing. She chose not to say anything. Clearly she was excited by the potential of this new relationship.

"All right, asshole." Ace was approaching from the bar. He was already loaded, even more so than usual. "You've been dating my wife for a week. Now you've gotten me fired. Way to go. Why don't you go back to England where you fucking belong before I kick the crap out of you?"

Gerald was more than a little startled. Ace was hardly conversationally threatening to Gerald, who was masterful at verbal sparring. But our Brit was a match for no one should it become physical.

"Come again, Ace? How exactly did I get you fired?"

"She wants me out—doesn't want me around to confuse things."

"She never told me that."

"Yeah, because of you she's feeling all confident about herself. She's ready to go out on her own again. She doesn't want me around anymore to cramp her style. So I'm out."

"Just like that?"

"Just like that."

"So what will you do now?"

"How the hell do I now? I've been unemployed now for forty-five minutes. I don't have any other skills besides making underwear."

"One more time," Gerald whispered to Cat. "Is that a skill or a deviant trait?"

"I heard that, asshole."

"Sorry, Ace."

"Are you going to be getting a divorce?"

"She never mentioned it, but I suspect it's coming at some point given how goddamned confident she's feeling right now!"

"I'm sorry to hear that, Ace." The Brit actually did seem to care.

"Yeah, well you're still an asshole."

"But we shouldn't let this get in the way of Libby's good vibes."

"Why? Is she dating my wife too?"

"No, but she's seeing another women she seems to like."

"And likes better than Will."

"Who the fuck cares?"

"He didn't really mean that Libby. We're all happy for you."

"I'm not sure I even understand what's going on here."

The dinner conversation at my house was never like this.

61.

"Why so glum, Libby?"

"I had a visit from her father."

"Ouch."

"He's a New York City detective."

"Tough guy?"

"Way tougher than I am."

"What did he say?"

"He said that if I saw his daughter again he'd report it to my boss and make sure I was fired."

"Can they fire you for being a lesbian?"

"Not anymore, but they can fire me for propositioning a recruit. It's bad form. I just couldn't help myself."

"I am sorry to hear that. Does that mean you and our man Will are going to be getting back together again?"

No answer. Although I have to admit it was hard to forget our near encounter in the latrine. That had almost been an incredible moment for me.

"So it's not so bad. You'll just have to find someone else."

"But I want her."

"You don't even know if she is gay."

"I'm willing to take that chance to find out."

"And risk your career?"

"Maybe I can become a banker."

"That field is already too crowded with the likes of me."

"How about I specialize in banking for lesbians?"

"Well, you might have something there. That is not a crowded market, I don't think."

With the exception of the army sergeant, we all had a good chuckle.

62.

"So Ace, glad to see you back on the train. We missed you."

"Like hell you did."

"How's the separation going?"

"You probably know better than I do."

"Look Ace, let's not lose our temper. Remember, I was trying to help you. It just turns out for the moment that your wife likes me better than she likes you."

"Asshole."

"Look, you're my friend. We can't let women get in the way of our friendship. If you want me to stop seeing your wife, just say the word."

"I don't want you seeing my wife."

"That's a little hasty, don't you think?"

"You said, 'Just say the word.'"

"Indeed I did."

"So?"

"Okay, I'll let her go."

"Just like that?" asked Libby.

"Why not?" replied the Brit.

His eyes and Cat's met, as they often did.

"You're going to break up for no apparent reason?"

"I have a reason. Ace told me so."

"You're harsh."

"That's what you said when I started seeing her."

"Well, you're even more harsh now."

Libby's eyes started to well up.

"Libs, dear, you can't be crying over my romantic life. It certainly isn't worth that amount of energy."

"Julie decided she's straight."

"Oh."

"Saddle up again, Will."

"Have some heart, Ace."

"I thought no one here had a heart."

"How do you know, Libby?"

"She told me she met a guy who she had feelings for."

"This is getting really confusing."

"Pay close attention, Ace."

"Who's the guy?"

"I don't know. All I know is he's married."

"Her old man's gonna pop a cork on this one too."

"You'll find somebody else, dear."

"What if I don't want anyone else?"

"Then there's always Will."

63.

Up until then Catherine had been the great mystery. While she easily fit in and was just as ready to slander someone as anyone else in our group, she was the one we knew least about. This probably had something to do with the fact, which I later learned, that she was easily the most complicated of our group—and even more messed up than Libby.

Libby did end up being suspended for her indiscretion with a recruit. And Ace set out to try to rebuild his career and his life with or without his wife. The commuter club was thus reduced to Gerald, Cat, and me—and I was certainly the outsider. Gerald would still get drinks from the bar, and Cat would match him strong drink for strong drink. Since the beginning the others had been the fodder for their piercing inquisitions. With just a threesome, we had to become acquainted with an uncertain new playground. I was just the video camera.

"So what are you going to do now without Her Majesty?"

"Oh, I expect I'll figure something out in due time. I've never been one to have long relationships."

"How come?"

"I don't know exactly. I probably feel they'll get to know me too well and realize me for the lazy, shallow drunk that I am."

"You're too kind to yourself."

They both had a good laugh.

"Did you like her?"

"I don't know."

"You don't know?"

"Not really. I truly had no intentions when I first started to see her other than helping out Ace. Clearly she hated him more than he'll ever know. But it's hard to say whether I was attracted to her or her lifestyle. She really is fabulously wealthy, you know."

"So why did you agree to stop seeing her? You have no love for Ace."

"Ace? Are you kidding me? He's like a long lost brother." They both had another good chuckle, and Gerald patted her on the thigh. Cat turned flush, though she tried her best to conceal it. I suspected it was a feeling that she had long ago forgotten. "Likely it was his sordid sense of honor. Ace is okay. He's just ugly when he's drunk."

"We have only seen him drunk."

"That's probably why I agreed to see his wife. I think somehow I felt sorry for the both of them. They were too drunk and too angry to recognize they were meant for each other."

They were silent for another moment.

"And who are you meant for, Gerald, the lousy but womanizing banker?"

"That is still to be discovered, Cat. Perhaps on another train ride. This is my stop."

"Will we see you tomorrow?"

"Indeed."

64.

GERALD WASN'T ON THE train ride home the next day. It was surprising given that he hadn't missed a single day the entire summer. So it was just Cat and me, which was a little strange given that she was probably about the same age as my mother.

"Well, Will, our gang keeps getting smaller and smaller. I guess it's just you and me tonight."

Cat had bought two plastic drinks. I had assumed one was for me. But she indiscriminately drank from each. So I guessed I was going solo on this ride.

"I'm okay with that, Cat. Hopefully I can be entertaining company for you."

"Well, the summer will be over soon, and you'll be heading back to school. I'll be back riding the train on my own again."

"I'm sure Gerald will be back tomorrow."

Cat paused before responding. I thought I noticed a little tear in the corner of her eye.

"I don't think so, Will. I think our little train gang has run its course."

Clearly Cat knew something I didn't. But I was much less comfortable with her than I had been with the others, so I didn't say anything. Plus, without the liquor I didn't have the same confidence.

So we sat in solitude for a few minutes and rocked with the train.

"How old do you think I am, Will?" She finally broke the silence, her drinks both empty.

"I'm not very good at that stuff, Cat."

"Give it a try."

I thought for a minute. She was strong physically and in personality. She was not gorgeous, but she was not unattractive. Her upper torso was broad and sturdy even without her substantial breasts. Like a swimmer whose shoulders have become overdeveloped with years of doing laps. Still, she had a bit of a gut. Not fat, but not thin either. Plenty of drinking with the boys had taken some of the curve away from her figure. Her strong thighs would likely squeeze the life out of anything they ensnared. Her aggressiveness was very sexy, even though she was old enough to be my mom.

Her hair was dyed a fake blonde, like most middle-aged suburban women that I knew, so it was hard to tell if there was much gray. But with the exception of small crow's feet around her eyes there were really no wrinkles on her face. I wanted to make sure I erred on the young side so as not to embarrass her.

"Thirty-seven?"

"You didn't want to embarrass me by guessing too high." She solemnly laughed. "I'm forty-eight."

I didn't say anything as she seemed to be talking to herself.

"I have a daughter I gave birth to when I was a junior in college who I subsequently gave up for adoption. I just met her for the first time two years ago. She wants nothing to do with me. I make four hundred and fifty thousand dollars a year as an attorney for a big corporate firm. Never met a deal I couldn't get done. Have a huge house with a pool, a home theater, and a workout room that collects dust. I got married for the first time when I was forty-four. He was a carpenter—I met him when he came to do work at my house. I kept dreaming up jobs for him to do so I had a reason to see him. He was so cute and so humble. He had the biggest heart of any person I had ever met. He was the first boyfriend I'd ever had.

"Timothy left me less than a year after we were married. Didn't want any of my money. He just couldn't stand me anymore. And I still loved him.

"Then Gerald touched my thigh the other night when we were riding home. I haven't been touched by a man in such a long time. I think it was something deep down I had been hoping I would get the chance to feel again.

"So I went over to his house last night. I thought up all kinds of reasons for being there, but the reality is that I just wanted to see him. I wanted him to touch me again. I wanted to feel that feeling again."

Now her tears were visible. But she paused.

"And?" I said softly.

"He has a nice, little Cape house in a nice family neighborhood. Perfectly manicured, as you might expect. He was still in his white dress shirt and suit pants but without the tie and jacket. He looked very relaxed and happy. Even more handsome than when in his full outfit."

"So that sounds promising."

"He was with Ace's wife."

65.

It had been almost exactly ten weeks since our group first met in the bar car of the New York–New Haven line. Together we had shared some of our most privileged feelings. At the same time, there was so little about each other we actually knew. We came to life on our hour-long excursion each day; we laughed, we cajoled, we taunted, we revealed feelings we never would have shared with friends or family. Never in a million years. Yet except for Cat's one unfortunate drop-in at Gerald's house we'd never seen each other outside of our bar car capsule. I guess she had broken the rule that had never been written.

Yet in due course I realized that all these people had flawed lives. My father would have flipped out if he'd learned that these had been my role models for the summer rather than the priests. The one thing I knew for sure was that I would miss my train gang.

They had made my summer interesting. They were the first adults I had ever interacted with and not felt guilty. It was a nice reversal to go about my life with a sort of confidence, not being afraid to say what I truly felt. I'd never really been able to do that previously. I was pretty sure that I would go back into my familiar shell once I returned to the Pendy campus, but at least for a little while it was a nice change. And, of course, I'd almost had sex. Even though Libby ended up being gay, which wasn't great for my self-esteem, it was as close as I had ever been.

So I was sorry to see my summer after junior year come to an end. I had nothing to look forward to at school my last year. More classes, more homework, no basketball. I would have to make an attempt at applying to colleges, but given my record I couldn't see how any decent college would want to let me in.

I decided I liked living on my own—priests or no priests. I liked the freedom of thought and action. I hadn't watched television or played a video game the entire summer. But it would still be nice to see my family. And I sensed that I was better prepared to handle whatever my parents threw at me.

"Hi, Will."

"Hey, Mom!" I always liked getting calls from my mother. She was so easy to talk to.

"You actually sound happy to hear from me."

"Yeah. I actually miss you guys."

"You aren't just saying that because you're supposed to, are you?"

"Naah. For dad I would, but not for you."

"I'm looking forward to having you home next week."

"Me too."

"It's kind of quiet around here without you."

"Try living in a rectory. When someone sneezes, it's a big event."

"How's your thesis coming?"

"Actually, not bad. I'm pretty close to done."

"Really?"

"Yeah. I kind of found some extra energy over the past month and put a lot of hours into it."

Actually, I wasn't faking it. I had worked on the paper rather than pretended to work on it. It felt good to be able to tell my parents the truth for once. Over the last month of the summer, I had picked up some newfound momentum in getting my punishment thesis completed. Since the train gang had given me the idea to write about me, it came fairly easily. After all, I was becoming a relatively interesting person. And since I usually had quite a buzz when I got home from work at night, it was pretty easy to be creative.

"That's great. I'm proud of you."

"I kind of am too."

"Hey, listen. I'm calling about Carl."

"Does he miss me too?"

"I'm not sure. I don't have good news, though. Carl was arrested for soliciting a nine year old girl. It's not good."

"What?"

I couldn't believe it.

"I just talked to him a couple of weeks ago. Wanted to make sure he was doing his workbook stuff."

"Well, I suspect your lessons will be curtailed for a while."

"A nine year old girl?"

"It's very sad and very disturbing."

"He has two young daughters."

"I know he told you that."

"It's not true?"

"Not according to the paper. They believe he has been molesting this one girl who he has introduced around town as his daughter. The police think there might be a second."

"That asshole!"

"I know, Will."

"Sorry about my language, Mom."

"I understand, honey."

The phone call with my mom brought back a familiar confusion. I had liked Carl and had always sort of looked forward to our Sunday afternoon sessions. I actually thought I was doing a good thing. After I hung up with my mom, I didn't know what to think. He'd been clear with me about his purpose in learning how to read. It turns out it was all a charade.

My first reaction was to call and scream at him—like my dad always did to me when I did something he thought was stupid. But I recognized that since he was in jail it might be a little tricky to reach him. My second reaction was one of sadness. It was hard to stomach any concept of Carl abusing such a young girl, imagining the lifelong damage he was inflicting. Still, given the Carl that I knew, it was hard for me to believe that he had actually done this. I mean, he was a not very big, uneducated doofus—but I thought he was a doofus with a good heart. My third reaction, for some foolish reason, was that it would make for a unique college essay—tutoring a man who took advantage of little children. But that wasn't likely to help my already limited chances of admissions.

My last act of the summer was to pack up a copy of my thesis and send it to Jelly. I sent it to Laurel and Hardy's address with a note asking them to make sure she got it. For all I knew, she may have already been off at college doing freshman orientation stuff. I don't know why I wanted her to see it. Somehow I guess I felt that it would be the final chapter for us.

66.

As tough as that past year was for both my mental capacity and my relationship with Will, I truly missed having him at home that summer. When there was no school, he was a lot of fun to have around. We would do things like go to ballgames together, analyze the players, make fun of the fans, and just have a great time together. But during the school year a wall would develop between us. With each year of high school, the wall got higher. I'm not sure I could see over it anymore.

I think our decision to have him get a real job in New York and learn to fend for himself—under the guidance of some Jesuit priests—was the right decision. We thought it would help him develop some much needed self-discipline. Picking him up at the train station at the end of August, he just seemed to have changed.

More mature.

Class I

67.

LIKE ALL SUMMERS, THAT one came to an end too. For a long time I missed my temporary friends from the New York–New Haven line. Even more I missed the liberty I'd felt when I'd been with them. There was no accountability and no consequences for our words or actions. That was a world I could have been quite comfortable in.

When I returned home, I was back walking the same treadmill. I was entering my final year of high school and still didn't have much of a passion for anything. I continued to simply go through the motions. It was like that really old animated Christmas show they play on television each December in which Kris Kringle taught the once villainous Winter Warlock how to walk. "You just put one foot in front of the other," according to the song.

I kept putting one foot in front of the other in whichever way people pointed me. But I didn't seem to be going anywhere.

I hadn't had my dream the whole summer when I was in New York. I didn't know if that was because I was free from school or because the alcohol had kept my mind a little clouded when I went to sleep at night. But the dream came back again soon after senior year started. The only difference was that Dawson wasn't in school that year, and he wasn't in my dreams any longer either. His family had moved to Utah, where they were from originally.

He wrote me a letter right before the school year began. As I might have expected, his penmanship was as neat as any I had ever seen.

Dear Will—

You are going to have a new Pendy person sitting next to you in assembly this year. My parents decided that if they moved our family back to Utah, they would have a better chance of convincing me to become straight. They figure that they have a better support structure in the community here. I never realized that being gay was an affliction. But they sure seem to think it is.

I will miss our time together. While I know that you and I spent most assemblies listening to Abby hyperventilate, I truly did enjoy our time together. I now know that I surprised the heck out of you when I asked you to the prom, but you didn't laugh in my face or run away. Rather, you treated me with dignity throughout. And while much to my chagrin our relationship was never romantic, I did appreciate it for being a good, honest connection.

Hope the new person talks more than I did (but less than Abby). Who knows, maybe when you are a famous basketball player and I am a gay Mormon bishop our paths will cross again? I wish you the best and will miss you.

Your friend,

Dawson

I realized that I would actually miss Dawson as well. His asking me out was a minor issue and one that ultimately did not bother me. Instead, once I got to know him, I recognized that I liked his freshness. He was deeper than I was, and while I admittedly hadn't set the bar very high, I admired that about him. He had certain convictions—how he dressed, his connection with a higher being, his sexuality—and I respected him for sticking to them.

Still it was hard to believe I was a senior. I felt like I had just arrived at Pendy. School would undoubtedly be different, as it was going to be my first year without Jelly. As much as we had gone our separate ways after the Fort incident, she was still the single person who could actually kick-start me. Jelly could make me sprint. Not always in the right direction, but sprinting nonetheless. I would miss that. She had been my adventure in high school. But since all eyes were on me after burning down the Fort, it was probably safer for me without her.

As part of my probation I wasn't allowed to play sports my last year. I knew I wouldn't miss cross-country, but basketball was a different story. I couldn't argue with their logic. I was lucky not to have been expelled. So instead, I had to spend two hours after classes each day working in the admissions mausoleum xeroxing and filing applications. Back where I had started. I didn't mind the work, and it helped me overcome my trepidation of the oriental rugs and antique lamps. I would read many of the applications the parents had ghostwritten for their children as I organized them along with their teacher recommendations and grade transcripts in manila folders, preparing each to be reviewed by the admissions counselors.

It was not so long ago that I had been one of the snot-nosed kids trying to get admitted to Pendy. The applications would have been impressive as hell if I had believed half of them. The twelve year old music prodigy headed for the Boston Symphony Orchestra. The fourteen year old athletic behemoth who would single handedly turn around the winless football program. And, of course, there was the diversity kid who was going to come to Pendy on a full ride like Shaky, and like Shaky be written off long before graduation. These parents all wanted so much for their kids to be accepted even though they knew so little about the school beyond what the glossy propaganda said. But I read and xeroxed and filed until it was time to go home and sit in front of my Dell once again.

Three weeks into the semester, my cell phone rang while I was planted in the middle of the file room absently dreaming while doing my unexciting job. It was the call that rang in a new academic year for me.

"Hello?"

My voice was getting deeper. I didn't really sound like the old me.

"Will?"

"Yes."

"This is Janet Seideman."

I didn't know who that was.

"Who?"

"I'm Jelly's mother."

Laurel.

"Oh, hi."

"How are you?"

"Fine, I guess."

"Do you have a few minutes to talk?"

I had all sorts of time.

"Sure."

"Jelly says hi."

"Oh."

I wasn't pissed at Jelly anymore. The fire in the Fort turret already seemed like such a long time ago. But I wasn't sure I ever wanted her to know I was over it. I had spent more time connecting with her than anyone in my life up to that time. In fact I probably was still in love with her even though I didn't really know what being in love was. I just knew her at a different, deeper level. Or at least I thought I did. Until she ran.

"She showed me your book."

"What book?"

"Well, I guess it's really your manuscript."

"What manuscript?"

"*I'm Will.*"

"That's a paper I wrote for school."

"Pretty long paper, don't you think?"

Damn right it was long. One hundred eighty-six pages. It was longer than all the other papers I had ever written in my life combined.

"I guess I had a lot to say."

"Do you mind if I ask why you wrote it?"

"I had to."

"How come?"

"I almost burned down the Fort."

"So I heard. In fact, I read about that."

"You read my story?"

"The whole thing. Isn't that what a writer wants?"

"I'm not a writer."

"If I were you I'd think again. You're a pretty darn good writer."

"It wasn't meant for anyone else to read."

"I'm glad you gave it to her."

I'll bet she was glad.

I had written all that stuff about her daughter, including implicating her in the Fort fire. I expected that Jelly had never told her parents on her own. It wasn't that I was intentionally trying to get anyone in trouble. I had actually never even thought about that. It just seemed important to me that if I was going to tell my story, then I should tell the truth. Laurel and Hardy must have been pretty ticked.

"Sorry about all that stuff in there."

"Don't be. Your story is very real—and I suspect your perspectives are not all that different from many high school kids. You write from your heart. That's the reason I called. You see, I'm a literary agent. I connect writers with publishers so they can get their manuscripts printed and onto bookstore shelves. I've been doing this a long time, and this is better than anything I've seen in quite a while. I want to help you publish it."

"Publish it?"

"As in make it a book."

"My parents haven't even read it."

"You should show it to them. They'd be very proud of you."

"I think they might kill me."

"I doubt that."

"You haven't met my parents."

"So are you interested?"

"In publishing *I'm Will?*"

"Yup."

"I've never in my craziest dreams considered it. And I've been known to have some crazy dreams."

"I read about that too. But it would be a crime not to."

"I mean, Laurel—er, Mrs.—Seiduh—"

"You can call me Janet."

"Sorry about that."

"Not a problem."

"You really think someone would want to publish it?"

"I actually think a lot of people would. It has a fresh and honest voice. And it's a hard story to put down. I read a lot of manuscripts, and I stayed up the whole night reading this one."

I'll bet you did. You saw a whole new, not so good side of your daughter.

"Can I think about it?"

"Why would you want to wait?"

"I don't really know. You kind of caught me off guard, I guess. I never really thought of it as a book."

"And you're worried that if someone publishes the book, then your parents will have to read it. And they never knew about any of the stuff you wrote about."

"Bingo."

"And you make your father look like an ass."

"Bingo again."

"Well, all I can say is imagine how I felt. Remember, Jelly's my daughter."

"Fair point."

This was all so inconceivable. I still couldn't grasp why someone would want to publish *I'm Will*. Hell, I was just hoping that I would get a passing grade on it and not get booted out of school.

"I still could use a little time to think about it. Would you mind if I took a couple of days?"

"Of course not. But don't take too long. You have a winner here. The money might be good."

"They'd want to pay me to publish my story? Are you sure?"

68.

"What did you do?"

"Pretty neat, huh?"

It was late, and I was calling on my cell phone in my familiar, distressed whisper. I still had Jelly as the first number on my auto dial—ahead of my mom and my dad, who were the only two other numbers I had programmed. I hadn't punched Jelly's number since the previous spring, when the Fort was still in good repair.

"Laurel works for a literary agency. I showed it to her."

"If my parents read this, they'll kill me!"

"What happened to 'Hi, Jelly, how are you?'"

"Your humor doesn't work anymore. I'm a dead man!"

"Who cares? You'll be a famous writer by then. Isn't that what they wanted? I believe 'initiative' was the word they used."

"You don't understand. They don't know that I did any of this stuff!"

"Oh, don't be so naïve! They're smarter than you give them credit for."

"I don't think so!"

"Hey, how do you think I feel? Half the stuff you wrote in the book is about me. My parents now know the true story that I was the one who actually burned down the Fort but was a chicken and ran and left you holding the bag. They know about my confused sexuality. Hell, you even described my left breast."

So finally the truth.

In my heart I had never totally believed Jelly was a lesbian. I had been hoping that she would eventually choose me. Until the fire in the Fort. After that I wasn't certain she deserved me.

"Yeah, but you like that stuff. Living on the edge. Remember, I live in a television rerun."

It wasn't taking the whole blame that had been so tough. I could handle the punishment. I would miss basketball, but the admissions work had its moments. I liked reading about all the kids and seeing how their parents had polished their applications for them. I had read enough of them by that time that I could tell which were real and which had been fabricated by the adults. But Jelly was supposed to have been the strong one. She was brash and bold. She didn't care what others thought. She was the rock. I certainly wasn't. And yet she bailed without hesitation.

"Okay, so you're right. But tell the truth. It's still pretty flattering. You're a high school senior and someone wants to publish your book. Laurel may be a shitty mother and wife, but she's an incredibly well connected agent. If she backs a book, it gets published, and it gets a lot of press."

"Press?"

"Yeah. You know. Talk shows, book tours, signings at Barnes & Noble. The authors from her last three published books have been on the *Today* show. I suspect Matt Lauer will want to interview you."

"Shit."

"Maybe they'll interview me with you. Wouldn't that be a hoot?"

"You can go on solo."

"But then I'll have to talk about your cute ass."

"Let's not go there."

"This could change your life."

"My life didn't need that much changing."

"I thought you hated high school."

"But that doesn't mean I want this much change."

"Well, I suspect it's coming whether you like it or not. Remember, I told you I would make it up to you."

69.

"Nervous?"

"I haven't felt this nauseous in a long time?"

"Since your first week of school?"

"I forgot that was in the book."

I was backstage and about to go on the *Today* show. Apparently someone at the network had read my book and liked it. Some staffer had called Laurel and sent tickets for us to fly to New York to appear on the show. This time I was dressed in a tie and jacket, but it wasn't the Pendy uniform. My parents had bought me some new clothes. The school was happy to give me the day off.

"You'll do fine."

"I still keep slipping and wanting to call you Laurel."

"If your book sells, I think I'll be able to get over it."

"How come you became an agent?"

"I've wanted to be a writer since I was a kid. I just never had your gift."

"I've never gotten better than a 'B minus' in English."

"We all overpaid for that school."

"Have you talked to Jelly lately?"

"Yeah. She called last night for Susie's and my anniversary."

"Funny, I never knew her name was Susie."

"Parents have names too, you know."

That was a comment for later.

"How is Jelly?"

"She's happy. She's likes the freedom of college and seems to be doing well. She says she has a boyfriend. I guess he's kind of an athlete. From Nebraska, of all places."

"I'm happy for her."

"She's still grateful to you for making her a minor celebrity."

"We had an interesting relationship, that's for sure."

"She's never talked about it."

At first Laurel's comment surprised me. But, in retrospect, what else could Jelly have added that the book hadn't already told? *I'm Will* had memorialized our relationship for others. I will admit it was amazing to see my story, the one I'd written while living with a bunch of priests as punishment for burning down the Fort, in print. Jelly had shared more details with Laurel about my clandestine yearbook photos, and Laurel had worked with the publisher to use some of them on the front and back covers. Photography had turned out to be a useful class after all. Jelly had also made sure her picture was included, even though I had never taken one of her.

I should have been concentrating on my first ever television appearance. It's funny that I actually wasn't. Instead I found myself thinking about the last four years and whether or not I had actually changed at all. Whether I was actually growing up. My life was out there for anyone who wanted to see. I might sell a few books, and it was pretty cool to be a published author. They couldn't take that away from me, like they had basketball. And while some of the stuff was more than a little embarrassing, it was at least honest. That made me feel pretty good. But I fully expected my book would be sitting on bookstore shelves in a few months collecting dust like so many others from more promising writers than me. So then what?

My life had been impacted by a relatively small number of people in what, in retrospect, seemed meaningful ways at Pendy. It occurred to me there weren't many loose ends to tie up. I was fairly certain that I would never see Dawson again. I hoped that he would find a way to come out of the closet. Unfortunately, it would probably forever ruin his relationship with his parents, which was too bad. He was a good person. And his goodness had helped me to reexamine my views on the possible presence of a higher being, which may have previously been a little short-sighted.

I had learned from Mr. Bussmann how fleeting life can be, not that this is what he had intended. Buzzsaw was gone for good. I would never need to have an awkward conversation with him at a Pendy reunion, although I doubted that I would ever attend one. But I knew I was not afraid of dying. It happened to the best of us, and I certainly wasn't among the best. My greater fear, as my dream kept hinting at, seemed to be of my willingness to help myself while I was still on this planet. To put forth the energy and determination to become a person with greater convictions. I didn't know if I would ever get over that fear.

Shaky showed me about family and how powerful a pull that can be. He was off following his own destiny. And while he'd been no more purposeful while at Pendy than I had been, his direction was nonetheless pretty well mapped out. Yet there was little chance that his future would ever overlap with mine because he would never be able to leave his grandmother behind. For all the angst my father had caused me, it would be interesting to see if I could ever leave my own family behind. It is what we, in the end, know better than anything else.

And then there was Jelly. I expected that when I was middle-aged with a job, a house and a family that I would still think about Jelly. We had connected in a rare way that I suspect most people never have the privilege of experiencing. I think she also knew that, and it scared her. Just like the fire in the Fort scared her. I might get in the way of Princeton and the myriad other future successes she'd likely planned for herself. She couldn't afford an anchor. Particularly one whose future was not projecting great promise. So she created a façade that was easy because her parents were lesbians. But Shaky was ultimately correct. Jelly and I were probably meant for each other but hadn't ever figured that out.

70.

AFTER THE SHOW, I told Janet that I was going to take the train back to Boston, and I think she understood. So I wasted a good amount of time wandering around Manhattan until the city's workday began to grind to end, at which time I headed for Grand Central for the first leg of my trip. I boarded the New York–New Haven train just as I had all that summer before. I was one of the first to board the train, habits being hard to break. My old orange seat was still there, unoccupied and waiting for me one last time. I had four copies of *I'm Will* in my backpack, genuinely hoping I might see some of my summer friends.

I sat and watched as commuters streamed by, wearing the same suits, jewelry, and gadgets that had become so familiar. As it was the end of the day, many with loosened neckties and rolled up shirtsleeves quickly began to line up at the bar. Ever since I knew I was coming to the city I had been looking forward to riding the train home. I wanted to feel that familiar fuel of the liquor and the conversation. I looked as each new patron entered the bar car, hopeful that each new face might be one I recognized. But sadly none of my train gang showed up. The cranky doors eventually closed, and the train lurched forward, beginning once again to repeat its nightly journey out of Gotham.

I felt empty sitting there alone. The sounds of the train remained familiar, as did the view of the landscape out the windows of the moving compartment. Without my old friends, however, there was no energy, no entertainment. So I closed my eyes and decided to revisit those days from not so long ago.

"Well, I guess you took us up on our idea after all."

I quickly opened my eyes and turned toward the familiar British accent and saw the double-breasted suit and the two pink cheeks. "I actually never knew your last name until I read the book."

"Where did you come from? I was watching every person who entered to bar car."

"I no longer drink on the train. But I thought that might have been you I saw through the doorway from where we boring suburban commuters ride. Thought I might come check to see if it was."

"I was hoping that I would see some of you guys tonight. That's why I took the train."

"Well here I am. I must say, Will, it seems you've been quite busy. The day I heard of your book—from Ace, in fact—I had to run right out and buy it. Spent most of the day reading while hiding it amid papers on my desk. It's quite an interesting story, you know. Have you sold quite a lot of them?"

"I don't think that it will ever be on a bestseller list if that's what you mean."

"Well, I guess you have to begin somewhere. And it sure seems like a pretty good start. I saw you on television this morning. By the way, I see that you've finally upgraded your wardrobe. Frankly I was getting a little tired of the blue blazer that was too small for you, and the khaki pants that were all worn out."

Gerald was smiling the whole time he talked. The only difference was that he didn't have a drink in his hand; his eyes were clear of alcohol.

"Do you still see the others?" I asked.

"Not on the train, anyway. My guess is that your book taught us all a lesson. Turns out we're not very nice people. Not very good role models, huh? Too much drinking, promoting sex with underage boys, committing adultery right in front of our friends. I suspect we were too embarrassed to recognize that when we were together."

"That wasn't my intent in writing this. I thought you guys were great."

"It's not your fault. You were the lens that showed us our self-absorbed lives."

"So you haven't seen any of them?"

"Actually I've seen them all. Ace's wife broke up with me before I would have, out of habit, dumped her. Ace was a better man than I, and I told her and Ace as much. I went to Cat's house to apologize. There was no romantic attraction on my part, but that was no excuse for my behavior."

"Wow."

"Yes, and now I'm dating Libby. It may be the first time in my life I'm truly in love. I hope she feels the same way."

"She's not a lesbian?"

"I suspect the jury's still out, but I hope not."

"Believe me, I know the feeling."

"Yes, I remember. You know, Will, it's quite a book."

Gerald, Ace, Cat, and Libby. Four grownups who, despite all being screw ups, managed to do just fine. Maybe it was okay not to be perfect. Maybe good grades and SAT scores were overrated.

71.

It's HARD TO FACE your dad when you've put in print a story that presents him in a not so complimentary way. I guess that over the course of the four years I increasingly recognized how much he had wanted me to succeed. But being at a school where I was in way over my head academically was really hard. Being in love with a lesbian was really hard. Not quite being certain that I had figured things out sexually was really hard. And not having anyone to talk to about all of this was really hard. He gave it everything he had. We were just on different wavelengths.

I would have been embarrassed as hell if I'd been him. I had laid out for the world the crappy job that he had done raising me, and yet everywhere he went he was boasting about me. He told everyone he knew or didn't know about my book. This wasn't what they had planned for me. It certainly wasn't the normal path of going from Pendy to a great college and on to business or law school and a life of big houses, nice cars, and interminable drudgery. But by pure luck I turned out not to be the total failure that he had feared. In fact, my failings had by some twisted fate caused my modest success, however fleeting it may end up being. But man, was he proud.

I just couldn't see it.

72.

COMMON APPLICATION FOR ADMISSION

YALE UNIVERSITY

PERSONAL STATEMENT

This personal statement helps us become acquainted with you in ways different from courses, grades, test scores, and other objective data. It will demonstrate your ability to organize thoughts and express yourself. We are looking for an essay that will help us know you better as a person and as a student. Please write an essay (250–500 words) on a topic of your choice or on one of the options listed below. Also, please indicate your topic by selecting the appropriate option below:

1. Evaluate a significant experience, achievement, risk you have taken, or ethical dilemma you have faced and its impact on you.
2. Discuss some issue of personal, local, national, or international concern and its importance to you.

3. Indicate a person who has had a significant influence on you, and describe that influence.
4. Describe a character in fiction, a historical figure, or a creative work that has had an influence on you, and explain that influence.
5. Topic of your choice.

My problem is that all of the boxes were in some way appropriate. I figured that I would leave them all blank, and they could figure out which question fit best.

I'm Will. Really. Michael William Harrington.

It's a little strange to have to write about myself when a bunch of people have by now bought a book I wrote and have read my mostly accurate story about me. If you were one of them, you likely already know that my first date was with a lesbian and that later that year I punched a teacher who incorrectly thought I was cheating. There probably isn't much more that I can add.

While I am truly impressed by your amazing academic institution, I have to be honest when I say I haven't yet decided if I truly want to go to college. This last year has been an unexpected whirlwind. While my classmates were playing sports each fall afternoon, I worked in a filing room as punishment for burning down a building on campus as well as for all the things I did at school that the administration never knew about until they read my book. An unconsidered result of pretending to be a writer, I guess.

On the other hand, the night my classmates were at our Christmas semi-formal dance I was being interviewed on live television (not that I would have necessarily had a date). Who would have thought?

I can't promise I won't write another book if I go to your school. My agent (a humorous concept) is angling for me to do so. Of course, that is how she makes her living. And I suspect that four years of college would provide plenty of material.

But for now I am asking you to consider my application with no promises from either side. I can't promise that I will accept if offered the chance to attend your fine school, and you can't promise I will enjoy my years there. Sounds like a fair deal to me.

About the Author

W.D. Haylon currently lives outside of Boston with his wife and four children. After many years as a fully engaged entrepreneur, he redirected his energies to becoming stay-at-home dad (where he has learned many things he never knew) and writing his debut novel, *I'm Will*. He is a graduate of Williams College and Harvard Business School.

You can visit him at www.williamhaylon.com